SANTA VS KRAMPUS

JIM HODGSON

CHAPTER 1

D aniel thought the building was being infiltrated by a SWAT team. The glass over the suburban mall atrium smashed, and dark figures began streaming down the wall like cockroaches. He realized that the figures weren't descending feet first on ropes like he'd seen SWAT team guys do in movies, but climbing on the actual walls, head down. Were they ... human? His mind fought the information his eyes were reporting.

There was nothing human about the oily black skin, the long arms and legs, the bared yellow teeth like daggers.

As he watched, the beasts — whatever they were — sprang off the walls and began streaking across the smooth floor toward him. His mind abandoned all processes except to think: *I am going to die in my green tights and green elf costume.* He was not afraid. He skipped right through fear into the certainty that he was going to die. It was calm, dreadful. The yellow teeth protruding from those mouths had to be as long as a man's forearm, and the claws were as big as railroad spikes.

The mall Santa leapt out of his red plywood chair with its

fake fur trim and withdrew what looked like a snow globe from a pocket of his robe. He extended the arm with the globe in it toward the nearest beast, then bellowed a word that sounded like-

Daniel thought idly that it must be a word from some ancient language, because why would anyone yell the word he thought he heard. The word sounded like, "Cock!" But why would anyone yell that at that moment?

Green fire shot out of the bauble toward the nearest charging monster, and struck it in the lower left part of its chest. The beast went down. The Santa corrected his aim to be a bit more on center, and a second gout of fire turned the beast into a meaty husk. The Santa whirled this way and that, directing the beam at the charging things one by one and dispatching them, turning them into a rain of repulsive black ichor, bones, and viscera.

Later, when he had time to think over what he was seeing now, Daniel would realize the beasts charged over or around the hapless mall shoppers, occasionally knocking one over, but didn't seem particularly concerned with attacking regular people. But he wasn't processing that information currently. His mind was occupied with being torn to ribbons in the next few moments. He couldn't even move.

He tried moving his legs. They responded, finally, though they felt like logs. He was backing slowly away from the destruction when his heel hit a plywood box painted to look like a present. He went over backward, cracking his elbow painfully on the cash register station. He landed hard. As he turned back toward the Santa — "Randolph," he'd said his name was Randolph Twisleham — the man was glaring this way and that. He appeared satisfied that he'd killed all the charging beasts, and was about to put the snow globe thing back in his pocket.

But from Daniel's low angle he could see that there was a beast sneaking up on the Santa from behind his Santa throne.

"Look out, Santa!" Daniel yelled, not remembering at the time the correct name to yell.

He yelled too late, though, because the beast was already springing powerfully through the air. It was huge! It jumped clumsily, clipping the Santa throne on the way past. The throne slammed into Randolph, knocking the snow globe from his hand and sending it rolling toward Daniel. Daniel grabbed for it, reflexively, then looked up to see the beast thing had recovered, and was stalking toward Randolph for another lunge.

The snow globe thing was heavy and cold in Daniel's hands. He watched helplessly as the beast's muscles coiled, prepared to spring. He held the bauble out toward Randolph, but was much too far away to do any good. The beast was moving between him and the Santa. The monster was enjoying this. It opened its jaws wide and roared at Randolph, then leaped.

"Shit!" Daniel screamed, an act of impotent fear. But as he did, a gout of fire erupted from the snow globe. It cut through the leaping form of the attacker like a blowtorch through a bag of spaghetti sauce, sending gore flying. Randolph managed to dodge the decapitated head of the monster, but was covered in its stinking black blood and entrails. The jaws of the monster's head worked a few times on the smooth mall floor, slowed, and were still.

Randolph picked himself up, gave a quick look around the scene at the wrecked Christmas decorations and shoppers yelling to one another, then strode over to Daniel.

"Give me that now, boy, and I'll explain in due course," he said. "We've got a bit of cleaning up to do first." He held out a hand, and Daniel placed the snow globe into it.

"What was-" he said, but Randolph cut him off.

"In due course," he said, then sighed, "I suppose this means I owe you my life, or some such. I'll never forget it."

He turned away then, still speaking but trailing off. Daniel thought he heard the phrase "pain in the ass," but couldn't be sure.

Whatever he'd said, he was as good as his word. He never forgot.

CHAPTER 2

Daniel took the job as a seasonal associate at the mall for the same reason anyone takes a job like that: because no better job will have them. He was a college kid who didn't have anywhere to go over the holiday break. Without a job, he also wouldn't have anything to eat.

It wasn't exactly true to say that Daniel didn't have anywhere to go. He had a home to go back to, but that would be like, well, it would be like going backward. He'd only just gotten out of home when he came to school. If he were asked to choose between going home over break and being dipped in a vat of boiling oil instead, he'd have asked to dip a toe in the oil just in case it wasn't quite boiling.

His parents were fine. They'd adopted him when he was a newborn. They raised him like their own. But at school he had his own room where he could do whatever he wanted.

Actually, as Daniel was thinking this, he realized that as an only child, he definitely had his own room at home, and he had a roommate at school, so maybe home was the better choice. But no. It wasn't. He was in college now, plenty old enough to be on his own. And anyway, he needed time to think; time he wouldn't get at home with his mom fussing over him, making sure he was fed, asking about his school work.

Half his first year of college was already gone and he had no idea what he wanted to do with himself. He felt like a dam sometimes, except instead of water he was holding back a gigantic pool of energy. The only problem was he had no idea where he wanted to put that energy. It was extremely frustrating.

Once, when he was a kid, there had been a grease fire in the kitchen. His grandfather was frying some chicken and the grease caught fire on the stove. Daniel had been sitting at the breakfast table at the time. When the flames began to lick up toward the cabinets, he'd bolted out of his seat, grabbed the small fire extinguisher his parents kept under the sink, and put the fire out. For those few seconds of action there had not been a thought in his brain. He'd just acted.

He loved that moment. He'd seen a problem, leapt toward it, acted decisively, and solved the problem while his grandfather was standing there with his hands on his head. He had the sense that he had what it took to help people, to be one of those people who runs toward trouble, not away from it.

Of course, he'd also once slammed his own fingers in a car door accidentally, but he didn't care for that memory as much.

He didn't know where he could fit in to develop his talent, if he had one, for leaping to danger. He didn't want to be in the military. He felt politics were confusing and distastefully nationalistic. Joining the police was out. He thought he could be a fireman, but had heard that it was hard to get accepted as one and didn't relish the idea of being up all night in a firehouse in any case. So what could he do? He had no idea, but he planned to spend his free time during the winter break trying to figure that out.

But because the school would be running on a limited crew while most students were away, he wouldn't be able to eat breakfast or dinner in the cafeteria, just lunch. He'd asked his mom for some money to get him through the break. She said if he just came home he could eat there. He faced a choice: go home and eat for free at his parents' house like a little kid, or stay at school, make his own way, and wrestle with his life's direction like a man. He strapped on his big boy pants and decided to do the latter, wondering to himself why "big boy" necessitated straps.

His mom wasn't happy. In fact, she cried a little, but she didn't make him come home. Dad just said he was old enough to make this choice and he hoped he'd considered the consequences. Daniel felt guilty because Mom was sad, but also excited. This exchange meant his parents recognized, at least, nominally, that he was no longer a child.

As far as the consequences, he did consider them. He considered them every moment of his life. If he didn't find some kind of a direction he'd feel dammed up like this for the rest of his life, which would surely mean he'd go insane.

In the meantime, while he wrestled with it, he needed some money over break or he'd starve.

He started his job hunt at places that sounded fun: a couple of record stores, even though he only listened to digital music files; a guitar shop, even though he didn't know how to play. He applied to a couple of coffee shops even though he had vowed never to work in the food service industry. Seeing other people's half-eaten food grossed him out.

The guy at the guitar shop said he could maybe use someone, but that Daniel would need to submit a resume with a cover letter. A cover letter!

"What does the cover letter need to have on it?" Daniel asked.

The man scratched his beard, then said, "Well, I'm not sure, but I took a small business owner's class, and that's what they said to ask for."

This sent Daniel down a well-worn avenue: Lack of Purpose Anxiety Avenue. Putting aside the cover letter, what would he put on a resume? Video games? Sleeping? Crap. He figured he could fudge something, maybe. People do this all the time right? He'd done some volunteer work before. That was something, right?

He thought he might be able to get a passable resume together, but the cover letter stumped him.

"Hi. My name's Daniel, and I have been told to include a cover letter. Neither I nor you know why I need a cover letter, but because I am the potential employee and you are the potential employer, here it is. I guess?"

He gave up on the guitar shop.

He made an ass of himself at one of the record stores too. As he was filling out the application, he tried to make conversation with the dude behind the counter.

Hearing the song playing in the background, Daniel asked, "Who is this playing?" Networking, Daniel thought. I am networking. The dude looked at Daniel like he'd just suggested that they both eat week-old roadkill.

"It's the Beta Band, 'Dry the Rain,'" the dude said. Well, that's what his words said. His face said, "Which you would know if you had half the brains of a goldfish."

Daniel finished the application and handed it over, and then walked out of the store firm in the suspicion that the dude had gone ahead and filed his application in the trash.

So, yes. The job search was going horribly. Days ticked by with no luck. He finished up his exams and waved goodbye to his friends as they left for their homes or vacation. If he didn't find something fast, he'd be eating one meal a day during the cafeteria's limited hours, since he wouldn't have money to go anywhere else.

He had to resort to desperate measures. He had to sink lower than low. He had to try his luck at the mall.

CHAPTER 3

He thought it would be easy, getting hired at the mall. He expected to have trouble getting into the stores, his passage blocked by all the signs requesting seasonal help. As it turned out, he'd waited too late, and most stores had all the seasonal associates they needed. Damn it.

Then he spotted a sign. It asked for seasonal help, which was good. And it was a shop he hadn't seen before, which was kind of also good. The only problem was it was an underwear shop called Top Drawers. Ugh. He considered his options, then quickly remembered he didn't have any options. Was he willing to be Underwear Boy?

We do what we must.

He walked in the door. Right up front there was a display of women's underwear. At least, he guessed it was underwear. It looked like small patches of lace held together with string. He reached out to make sure they were actually garments and not just lengths of string, and at that exact moment a voice behind him said, loudly, "Can I help you?" He jumped and jerked his hand away like the panties had bitten him.

"I uh," he said. Standing there was the most beautiful girl he'd ever seen. She was a little shorter than him, with almost-white blonde hair, clear blue eyes, and a half smile on her face. Daniel got the sense that she'd startled him on purpose.

"You startled me," he said. His heart was thumping.

"I sure did," she said. It was weird, though. She said it like the two of them were sharing the joke, not like the joke was on Daniel.

He relaxed a little.

"So, can I help you?" she asked.

"Yeah, well, I'm looking for a seasonal job. I saw the sign."

"Do you have a lot of experience with underwear?" she asked. An eyebrow raised slightly.

"Sure do," he said. "I wear it every day." At this point he took a microsecond to let his brain know that it needed to be in the absolute topmost gear that it had. He couldn't have pinpointed why exactly he needed his brain in top gear, but he knew he wanted this woman to think he was smart.

"What about with women's underwear?" she asked.

"Is that what those are? I thought they were lace sling-shots." *OK, brain,* he thought. *Not bad. Keep it up.*

"Why would someone make a slingshot out of lace?"

"Exactly *my* question," He said. He made an exaggerated movement with his hands to help sell his confusion about lace slingshots and was rewarded with a little laugh. He followed it up with "What's your name?"

"It's Janika," she said, and pronounced it "Yanika." She spelled it for him.

"Wow, people must misspell your name a lot, huh?" he asked.

She sighed. "They do."

"Yeah, I get that a lot too. It's a drag."

"Oh yeah? What's your name?"

"It's Dan."

She blinked, so he spelled it.

"D... A... N..." he said, drawing each letter out.

She made another little laugh sound and reached a hand out, swatted him on the arm. "You're a nerd, D-A-N."

"No, seriously, it's a real problem." He didn't want to work at Top Drawers, but he was starting to think he might take a job anywhere Janika was going to be.

"Yeah, I bet. Listen, D-A-N Dan, I'm gonna tell you a little secret." She stepped closer, which he liked. She was wearing some kind of light perfume that he could have sniffed at for days. "You don't want to work here," she whispered, using a hand to shield her face, which was approximately the cutest gesture he ever saw.

"Oh no? Why not?"

"The owner is kind of hard to get along with. Most people quit within a few weeks." He was noticing she had a little bit of an accent. She didn't really pronounce the "th" sound in "the." She said it more like "dah." And her cadence was peculiar too. And by "peculiar," he thought to himself, he meant "super cute." He considered bringing her accent up, but decided it might seem more worldly if he ignored it, as if he spoke to people with accents all the time.

"So why are you still here? Sounds like a real jerk."

"Because he's my older brother."

Oops, he thought. "Oops," he said.

"Nah, it's OK. He's not really a jerk, he's just hard to read. And he's still a little new to retail, which puts him on edge a little bit. And he works out a ton, so he's very big, which intimidates some people." She put her arms out with fists pointing down to demonstrate bigness.

"Wow. A short tempered guy who's enormous, huh? Remind me not to get on his bad side."

"Oh," she said with a smile, "Once you see him, I won't have to remind you."

Daniel didn't know how to handle that one, so he just laughed.

"But I have good news for you," she said. "The mall Santa is hiring."

"Would I have to grow a fluffy white beard?"

"I don't know. But you might have to wear tights."

Yeah, right. Tights. Now he knew she was pulling his leg. "Not a problem for me, I have great legs. Besides, tights are just very long underpants, and I have lots of experience with underpants, as you know."

She laughed again, this time with her hand over her mouth. "Well, you should go apply then. And maybe I'll see you around."

Because he was a gigantic idiot, he said, "Maybe!" instead of something smooth like, "Well, why don't you see me around tomorrow when we go get a coffee together." Then he observed himself as though he were hovering outside his body. His waved, smiled, then walked out. As of three steps later, he was ready to kick his own ass for missing the opportunity to talk to Janika more. Why didn't he ask her out? Idiot!

Some fearless person he was.

But the good news was that she was right about the Santa thing. He spoke to a lady behind the cash register kiosk and she said they needed people badly. He could start right away. The not so good news was that Janika was, in fact, not kidding about the tights. Kiosk lady handed him a pair in a sealed plastic bag.

Well. He needed a job, and he wanted a reason to come back to the mall. Besides, tights are just very long underwear, right?

CHAPTER 4

The next day, Daniel showed up for work as an elf — or to use the phrase the mall used, "Xmas Seasonal Associate" — with the tights on under his jeans. The lady he'd spoken to about getting the job asked him to show up an hour before the mall opened. He didn't want to be late, since being late on your first day at a new job is among the dumbest of the world's dumb moves. Besides, he thought he might run into Janika on her way into Top Drawers.

He didn't see Janika, but he did see an enormous human walking toward the entrance. This person looked like a pile of rocks that had learned to walk. His shoulders were so wide that Daniel thought they were going to bust the glass doors apart as he walked through them. He figured this giant must be Janika's brother, unless there were two crazy huge stacks of meat working at this mall.

Daniel walked in behind him, maybe twenty feet back, then watched as the big man stopped at Top Drawers to unlock its metal bars. He squatted easily, almost gracefully, which was surprising for a guy of his size.

As Daniel passed, the giant turned his head. His brow pushed down on his face, and his jaw stuck out, giving him the look of a man extremely displeased with the world. Having spoken to Janika, Daniel knew to expect this guy to be somewhat mean-looking, but he was so big and was mean mugging so hard Daniel had the urge to apologize to him. But for what?

"Hey," he said instead.

The giant stood up, looked at Daniel walking by, then eventually gave a little nod.

Daniel thought: It's a start, right? And he'll warm up to me after Janika and I have been married a few years.

Then he felt a little weirded out that he'd just had a non-ironic thought about being married. Maybe he was still a little sleepy. Coffee would have to wait, though, because he'd arrived at the middle of the mall, where the Santa setup was.

There was a big red char, trimmed with faux white fur, and a large Christmas tree with brightly colored boxes underneath. The tree was trimmed with lots of lights, garland, and round red ornaments. The area was roped off, with faux green garland wrapped around the ropes. At the end farthest from the chair and tree was a kiosk, presumably where people paid for their turn to place their kids on Santa's lap.

"Why aren't you wearing your tights?" the lady he'd spoken to the day before asked from behind the desk. Joan. Her name was Joan.

He said was wearing his tights under his jeans.

Joan said, "Are you shy or something? Worried someone's gonna look at your little bum-bum?"

"My bum bum?"

"Your little cutie patootey?"

"P-uh. I, um." He shrugged. "I'm just not used to tights."

Joan grinned, seeming a little predatory. "I'm being kinda bitchy huh? Well, sorry. Welcome to Santa's Workshop. Come on, kid, we'll get you your smock." She turned and walked away from her kiosk then, and Daniel could see that she too was wearing tights under a sensible red dress. He couldn't have guessed her age. Definitely older than he was. Not as old as his parents, though she did have a certain mom-ish vibe about her. He'd never heard an adult her age describe themselves as "bitchy," except on TV. And wait a minute. Wasn't that kind of a bad word? He let that one go for now.

"A smock?" he asked, but she was walking away. He hurried to catch up. She led him through some double doors into a back hallway, then around a corner to a dressing room door.

"Hey, do I need to fill in a form or anything like that?"

"A form?" Joan asked.

"Yeah, you know, usually on your first day at a job you fill out a form, write down your social security number, that kind of thing?"

Joan made a sort of guffaw noise. "No, you won't need any of that right now." She said. She was smiling like she knew something he didn't.

"OK, well, what about my bank information? You guys do direct deposit, right?"

"Let me ask you something, kid," Joan said. She was close now. "You ever kissed an older woman?"

"Uh," Daniel said.

"I'm only 32, you know. You might be surprised. In fact, I can guarantee you you would be."

"I mean, uh," Daniel began. "You seem very nice, but this is like, a job, right? I don't think we um."

Joan laughed then, like he'd said something hilarious, then looked at him again, as if gauging his reaction to her laugh. She was an extremely peculiar person, Daniel thought.

"You're a riot, kid. Just poke your head in and make sure no one's in there to see your bum-bum," Joan said.

He poked his head in. Linoleum tile, taupe cinderblock walls, a sad-looking mirror and a battered folding chair.

"There's no one in here," he said, but Joan was gone.

She reappeared from a nearby door that must have been the ladies dressing room. She was holding something green in her hands. She held the green thing up in front of Daniel, then nodded and tossed it at him. "OK, there's your smock. Put that on and meet me back out at the kiosk. You can leave your things in the dressing room, but you probably don't want to leave your wallet. You never know, right?"

"I guess not," he said.

"You guess right," she said. "You never know."

CHAPTER 5

Wait, Daniel thought, I'm supposed to put this on? It looked like a dress for someone attending a Worst Holiday Cocktail Dress party. It was green felt with sequins glued on in various holiday shapes. One was a star. Another series of sequins wound around the side of the thing, but at first he thought it was just a series of weird blobs. Then he realized the blobs were meant to represent a toy train.

He looked up, hoping to see that Joan was pulling his leg and he wouldn't actually have to wear this atrocity in public, but she had disappeared down the hall. The smock looked positively hideous when he held it up and looked at it in the mirror, and the fact that the cheap mirror distorted his shape into freakish proportions wasn't helping.

Then he heard the door to the dressing room open. He whirled, expecting to see Joan there, probably laughing that she'd gotten him good with the hideous green smock or making more jokes about his "bum-bum."

Instead, there was a tall, impeccably dressed gentleman with a long white beard. He was wearing a pinstripe, double-breasted suit and carrying a garment bag. He looked like he'd come to this particular mall to show everyone who bought their clothes here what clothes were supposed to look like. He also looked a little tired.

"Oh, hello," he said. His voice was warm, and his English accent made him sound like a documentary film narrator. "You must be our new elf." He crossed the room, then stuck out his hand and shook Daniel's warmly. He smelled like cologne and leather upholstery, but there was also a faint whiff in there. Could it have been alcohol? At this time of day? Surely not.

"Well, I ah," Daniel said. He wanted to make a cutting remark about the horrific smock thing he was holding, but nothing was coming to mind. He looked at it in his hand. One of the glued-on sequins had come unglued and was now stuck to his palm.

"Perhaps we're a bit hesitant to wear the outfit?" the gentleman asked.

"It's a little," Daniel said, but ran out of words. "It's not what I usually wear."

"I should hope not. It's hideous," the man said, then laughed. Then he put a hand out, "I'm Randolph Twisleham. And you are?"

"Daniel. Daniel Norwich. Nice to meet you, Mr. Twisleham." They shook.

"Please, call me Randolph. When you see the absurd costume I'm about to put on, I assure you, any inkling of respect you might have had for me will evaporate."

He hung his garment bag on a hook and unzipped it. Daniel could see a bright red Santa Claus outfit peeking out of the bag. Randolph stripped down to his undershirt and boxer shorts without an apparent care in the world, then kicked his legs into a pair of fuzzy red pants with white trim and shrugged on a matching coat. He tugged on a pair of boots, humming a song Daniel didn't recognize as he did so.

Daniel took off his shirt and pulled on the smock, but couldn't wiggle his arms down the sleeves. Something was blocking them. He pulled at the material inside the sleeves, intending to straighten whatever snarl was inside. As he did, he withdrew a green felt bootie with jingle bells dangling from the upturned toe. Whoever had worn this getup last had stuffed it down the sleeve. There was another in the other arm. Oh, God.

Daniel took off his jeans, revealing the tights, put on the smock, and looked at himself in the mirror as he pulled on the booties. They were too big, but the elastic in the heels helped some. He looked like he'd been dipped in green. He looked like a weird lamp shade. He looked-

Behind him, Randolph Twisleham said, "Ooh, my giddy aunt. I doubt anyone's ever laid eyes on two more garishly-dressed buffoons." He laughed then, like he'd heard the funniest joke ever told, and Daniel couldn't help but notice that his laugh had taken on a bit of a "Ho ho ho" quality that he hadn't heard before. The sound of it made Daniel want to laugh too, and he did.

"Can you keep a secret?" Randolph asked.

"It depends. What's the secret."

"It's drinking." Randolph said. "On the job," he added.

"In the morning?" Daniel asked.

"Probably," said Randolph. "But also right now." He withdrew a silver flask from his garment bag, unscrewed it, and had a long pull. He offered it to Daniel as well, who declined. Randolph then popped a mint in his mouth. "Jolly good," he said around the mint. "Let's see what these kids have got, shall we?"

With that, Randolph turned and strode out of the room, pulling the door open as if he was doing the hallway a favor by striding into it. He was weird. Definitely weird, Daniel thought. But he'd never met someone who didn't care at all if they looked ridiculous.

His attitude lifted Daniel. So much so that he almost felt proud to be dressed like a Christmas store had thrown up on him. He followed Randolph out the door and into the hall thinking this must be what it feels like to be a soldier with a very charismatic general.

They weren't striding into battle. They were just walking out into a suburban mall dressed as Christmas characters. But in that moment, surreptitious day drinking notwithstanding, Daniel would have picked up a sword and followed Randolph Twisleham into the slavering maw of the enemy.

Little did he know he'd get his chance to do exactly that.

CHAPTER 6

After the fight with the horrible dog-things, after the last one exploded in Randolph's fire and Daniel handed the globe back, Randolph searched the area. Daniel got up and dusted himself off. He found that he didn't have any wounds, other than his pride being injured at having fallen over on his ass and the knock to his elbow. Sparks of pain occasionally shot out of his elbow as though he was being electrocuted in that spot, but those seemed to be diminishing.

There was also still the embarrassment at being dressed like the world's least attractive Christmas-themed table lamp, but it registered only vaguely as Daniel's senses recovered from the past few moments' terror.

Randolph was going from mall shopper to mall shopper, inquiring whether they had any injuries, asking if they were OK. They all nodded that they were fine. Randolph showed each of them his snow globe, they looked into it then thanked him, waved goodbye, took their shopping and left.

Daniel trotted after him. When he caught up, Randolph

was on his cell phone, but ended his conversation and put it away.

"What's going on?" Daniel asked.

"I'm just reminding these people that they didn't see anything here."

Daniel looked around. A revolting dead thing lay nearby, its mouth was open in a snarl, its rear half disconnected from the front, a pool of oily black filth in between the two chunks.

Daniel pointed at it. "That's not anything?" He stepped aside so he didn't get any oozing black filth on his booties.

Randolph looked grave. "Right now it is something. And it's troubling. The memory of this little skirmish would irritate these people the rest of their days. Luckily I have just the thing for it." He withdrew the globe from his pocket, gave it a twirl, then dropped it back in.

"So you can erase people's memories?"

"Not exactly, no. It's more like cleaning out the trash. Nobody wants to remember unpleasantness. And these curs wouldn't fit into their reality anyway. It would be like a splinter in their brains, this memory. So we just pluck it out."

"That sounds like you can erase people's memories."

Randolph shrugged. "No memory is forever. I am merely hurrying the process along."

Randolph had already spoken to and dealt with the mall shoppers who had been in direct sight of the monsters. Luckily the mall wasn't quite open yet so there weren't many people around. He was heading in the direction of Top Drawers, though, just around the corner.

Daniel realized what was about to happen and ran to catch up again. "Wait!" he yelled.

Randolph stopped and turned to look.

Daniel said, panting though he'd only trotted a step or two, "You don't have to zap the people around here. They didn't see anything." A small voice in his head reminded Daniel that he had no reason to believe that having your memories erased or plucked out or whatever was anything other than a pleasant experience. The people he'd observed looking into Randolph's globe certainly seemed pleased. But for some reason, he didn't want Randolph to zap Janika. What if she forgot about meeting him?

On the other hand, that might give him a second chance to make a first impression with her. He could ask her out at their first meeting this time instead of blowing the opportunity like a dumbass.

Randolph was speaking. "I said," he said, "why shouldn't I?"

"Well, I. I think you, um..." Daniel stammered. "They're my friends," he finally managed to say.

Behind Randolph, someone giggled. Daniel craned his neck to see where it had come from, and there stood Janika with her gigantic brother, who was, as was apparently his custom, glaring.

"We'll be fine," she said, then added, "but that was so sweet." Then she smiled. Daniel smiled back. The giant glared. Daniel thought he might have heard a growling noise too, but that might just have been his imagination.

"Preliminary containment?" Randolph asked.

"We should be OK," Janika said. "Early morning. Not a lot of shoppers. We have the perimeter up and the team is inbound."

"Very good," Randolph said. "Well done, that woman." Then a moment later, he added, "...and man."

Janika's brother appeared to relax a little.

Since everyone seemed to be getting along, Daniel went over to the giant and stuck a hand out. "Hey," he said. "We haven't met yet. I'm Daniel."

"Oh yes," interjected Randolph. "Terribly sorry. Daniel

Norwich, meet Justus Prins. I gather you've already met Janika."

Justus put out a hand the size of a gift ham, with fingers the size of summer sausages.

Daniel was delighted to find, after the handshake was completed, that he still had a hand on the end of his arm. "Nice to meet you," he said.

"And you," Justus rumbled back, though his face didn't show any great pleasure. His accent sounded Russian to Daniel, but that couldn't be right if he was Janika's brother. Her accent was more German or something.

As Daniel was looking at him, Justus's eyes went to Janika, then back to Daniel. Daniel was not a mind reader, but he got the distinct impression that Justus seemed to be warning him to tread lightly where Janika was concerned or he'd pull Daniel's arms off, freeze them solid, and use them for salad tongs.

"Justus, be nice," Janika said, her voice light and musical. Then, to Randolph, "I don't suppose it much matters if we meet him or not, though, does it?"

"Not really, no," Randolph said.

"What?!" Daniel said, which was ignored by all present. "Wait a minute, you're going to wipe my memory?"

Randolph tilted his head. "I was going to, yes, but since you seem to have an aversion to it, I'll just have Justus snap your neck instead."

"It doesn't look big enough to make a snap," Justus observed. "Click maybe."

"Boys," Janika said.

"Oh all right. We're having fun with you," Randolph said. "We're not going to wipe your memory, as such. You'll remember lots of things. None of this, obviously, but lots of things."

"But, can't I go with you?" Daniel asked. The question

surprised him a little, especially in that it had come from his own mouth, but it whatever this crew was up to, it was a lot more interesting than his life had been up to now. Janika was definitely very, very interesting. She was smiling at him, something that women his age didn't do very often. Randolph was full of some sort of self-confidence that Daniel found hard to define but desperately wanted to emulate. Justus looked strong enough to close a door in a concrete wall by grabbing either side of the wall and simply pulling until the opening disappeared. Taken alone, any one of these people would have been the most interesting person he'd ever met. He couldn't just let them walk out of his life.

"Where does he think we are going? On a shopping trip to the mall?" rumbled Justus with a smirk.

Everyone looked around. Bright lights. Store signs. Open doors of mall shops.

"I admit, was bad choice of words," Justus said.

Randolph sighed. He looked from Daniel to Janika to Justus. "Why does everything have to be such a fantastic pain in the arse?" he asked.

CHAPTER 7

"I am quite sorry, Daniel," Randolph said. "I simply can't take you with us. If I were a Santa in good standing, things might be different, but in fact I am about to retire, you see. I only took this assignment today as a favor to-"

"Randolph," Janika said. She was looking at him pointedly.

Randolph frowned. He looked very angry. He drew in a breath to speak again, but at that moment a cell phone made an electronic jingling noise. He withdrew it from a pocket, moaned, and stepped away to answer it.

"Sorry about him," Janika said. "Randolph is from the old times, and he has old ways. If you have the ability to do what we do, he cannot refuse, even if it is uncomfortable for him."

"So if I can do magic, using his globe, then he has to let me go with you guys?" Daniel asked.

"Unless we just don't like you," Justus said.

Janika kicked Justus in the leg.

"Ow," he said, obligingly.

Randolph came back. "That was Washington. He's spotted something odd. We must go."

"What about me?" Daniel asked. "I used the globe, right?"

Randolph looked pained. He had no immediate response. "Shit," he said. A spark of light shot up from the top of his head.

"Yes, Randolph, what about him?" Janika asked.

Randolph glared at Janika, then looked away. "Shit again," he said. This time there was a spark and a puff of smoke just over the top of his head when he swore. It looked like someone was testing out an invisible disposable lighter an inch above his hair.

"Is anyone else seeing him shoot sparks out of his head?" Daniel asked.

"It's a side effect of having used magic for a long time. Emotions and words are tied very closely to magic. When Randolph is irritated, sometimes he sparks," Janika explained.

"And sometimes I drink," Randolph said.

"Using magic leaves us drained both physically and emotionally. Happens to everyone." Janika said.

"Not me. I have not had an emotion for twenty years," the Justus said. "I am a bottomless black abyss beyond an impossibly towering cliff."

Janika kicked him again.

"I feel pleasant breeze near my ankle," Justus said.

"What does any of this have to do with Christmas?" Daniel asked.

"Oh no," Janika said. "Now you've done it."

Randolph was visibly winding up to cover a topic he'd covered many times, like someone who was into caving explaining why "spelunking" isn't a word they use, or a cyclist explaining why bikes should be in the road and not on the sidewalk.

"Being a Santa has nearly nothing to do with Christmas.

In fact, the commercialization of Christmas is down to Krampus's evil influence," Randolph said. "We are wizards. Wizards! It just happened that in this case, we needed to plant ourselves in some local malls and being mall Santas is often a convenient cover."

"It's also a new Santa's first assignment," said Janika. "Like the way a policeman starts on the street."

Randolph gave her a sidelong glance.

"But you also call yourself a Santa," Daniel said. "And you're dressed like one."

"Damn it, it's complicated. But take my word as golden, we have nothing at all to do with Christmas. Nothing. At all. Now, if you'll just look into this snow globe, I-"

"Randolph," Janika said, in a voice that indicated she wasn't going to let something go.

Randolph glared at Janika. His eyes were like fire. His body tensed. Tendrils of smoke rose from his ears.

Janika was unperturbed by this display. "Well, let's get going," Janika said. "Come on Daniel, Randolph's just being peevish. Our order needs new recruits, don't we?"

"I don't like him," Justus said. "But I do not want to be kicked."

"But if you're a bottomless pit of whatever, you don't like or dislike anything," Daniel said.

"You might have point, but as bottomless pit, I am not caring," Justus said.

"You really have some nerve, girl," Randolph said. He gave the resigned sigh of a man who thought he was going to ignore and bluster his way through a conflict and has failed.

"I did have some nerve, when I was a girl. And I do now that I am a woman as well," Janika said, levelly.

Randolph had the grace to know when he was outmaneuvered. "Oh, very bloody well," he said. "Let's go then. We must hurry."

Daniel felt his heart leap in his chest. "Will we be going in a sleigh?" he asked.

"Oh, don't be ridiculous," Randolph spat. "We'll take the Jag."

Figures in red coverall suits were running up behind Randolph. Daniel tensed, fearing another attack of some kind, but no one seemed perturbed as they approached, so he tried not to freak out. One of the men called to Randolph that containment was in progress and the perimeter hadn't been challenged.

"Hey, who are these guys in the suits? What are they doing?" Daniel asked as they strode toward the mall entrance.

"Oh. They're a containment team," Randolph said, pushing open the doors to the outside. Janika and Justus trailed behind. "They'll clean up the carcasses, fix anything that's broken, and make sure the mall is exactly as tiresome it was before the curs attacked."

"What's a cur?"

"In general it's a name for any dog that's aggressive or in poor condition, but in this case I'm using it to refer to Krampus' curs, which are, it must be said, both. It's what we call those revolting beasts."

"They're called Krampus curs?" They were outside now.

"Krampus's curs," Randolph said, enunciating clearly.

"Oh. Who's Krampus? Are the curs named for him because he discovered them, like Thomson's gazelles?" Daniel thought that was a particularly smart question to ask. He knew to ask it because he'd just learned about Joseph Thomson and his gazelles at school.

"Something like that. Are you familiar with Krampus?"

Daniel shrugged. "Yeah, he's like, the Christmas devil or something like that."

Randolph frowned and wiggled his head to indicate that it could be considered something like that. "There are myths about him that originate in the deep woods in Northern Europe, yes."

"So why are those curs named for an imaginary Christmas myth guy?"

"Oh, he's not imaginary. They're named for him because he summoned them, or created them. We don't know which. They are his minions. And they, like us, have nothing to do with Christmas."

"Right," Daniel said. "Next you'll tell me Santa Claus is real too."

"He is, of course, although Santa Claus is a title, not a name. The last Santa Claus was female."

Daniel looked over his shoulder. Janika and Justus were a few steps back, talking to one another, not paying attention. "What's up with Janika and Justus?" Daniel asked.

"What do you mean?"

"They're brother and sister, but their accents sound different to me,"

"Ah, yes. They are blood relations, but grew up apart, adopted by different families."

"Oh," Daniel said. "I was adopted, too."

"Yes," Randolph said.

Daniel thought that was an odd thing to say at that moment, "yes," But he let it go, thinking it must be a peculiarity of English gentlemen with which Daniel was unfamiliar, having never chatted with any English gentlemen or Santas before.

"Right," Randolph said as they approached his car. "Everyone in."

CHAPTER 8

I n another corner of the parking lot, Joan concentrated on walking calmly. *I'm just a regular mall shopper*, she thought. *I don't see the men in stupid red suits. I don't know of anything that happened here at all other than the normal morning business of a suburban mall opening. I am positively, definitely not involved in anything that could be considered "espionage."*

She could see her car now. Almost there. The urge to look over her shoulder was rising like an itch between her shoulder blades that was lengthening, crawling up her spine to become an itch on the back of her head.

Now she could see herself reflected in the glossy black paint of the long sedan. God, how she loved this car. She opened the door and reveled, as she always did, in the professional quiet click of the door latch opening, the silky smooth action of the hinges, and the stately thud and click as it shut again behind her.

Safe behind her tinted windows, she looked around. No one. No one had followed her. She was in the clear. She felt like she might throw up, but to her surprise, she giggled. She'd done it! She hadn't been sure she could.

Then she let out a heavy sigh, and to her surprise, felt a tear rolling. The feeling that she might throw up rose again. She cried for a moment, then wiped her eyes. What were those awful things that had come through the skylight?

Truth be told, she wasn't sure exactly what she'd done, but she'd still made it out, which seemed like success.

She dug her cell phone out of her new handbag. The handbag, like her car, was a thing of beauty, but also of taste. She'd known, her whole life, that if she ever had real money she'd know exactly how to spend it. Expensive things? Of course. But tasteful too. Tasteful things.

The cell phone was bigger than her hand and she wasn't used to it so she fumbled with it. She managed to get it to dial the number, though.

A voice answered. A male one this time. "Yes?" it asked, drawing the word out.

"It's done," she said. "But the kid left with the old man,"

There was a pause. The pause lengthened. Was anyone still on the line?

"Hello?" she asked.

"I'm afraid you'll have to be more specific," the voice said. It really liked to draw words out, didn't it? It sounded like someone doing an impression of an old butler or something.

She had a fleeting thought: Butler? Could I have a butler? Maybe an assistant? She'd worry about that later. She refocused.

"It's done," she repeated. "I hired the kid. He came to work this morning, and then the ... things came. I was expecting lawyers, not whatever the hell those things were."

A long pause again. This time she just waited for the voice to respond.

"Yes?" it said. A question? She hadn't expected that. Did it mean for her to go on?

"Yes, and ... well, the Santa Claus man killed all the dog

things, but then they left together, the Santa man and the boy, plus some girl and a big muscle guy."

"And where were they going?"

"I don't know, I-" there was a click as the voice hung up. She held the phone away from her face and regarded it with surprise. It changed its screen from the one it showed when it was a phone and went back to the lock screen. She put it down.

How rude. What did this mean? Should she call back? Had they been disconnected? She didn't get that feeling. It definitely felt like she'd been hung up on.

She'd taken this assignment after being — well, there was no other word for it — recruited. She'd been unsuccessfully looking for work in public relations. She'd gotten an email complimenting her on her resume, and assumed it had come from someone who had seen her on one of the job sites where she posted regularly.

If you listed your email address in your post, sometimes employers would email you directly so they didn't have to deal with the recruiting message board thing. She'd read that online, so she'd put her email in her listing.

She'd gone to meet her mysterious email correspondent in an office building in the suburbs, northeast of town. He'd promised her an unbelievable sum of money if she accepted the position, with the understanding that she'd be asked to engage in what he called "intra-company work," which she understood to mean some sort of corporate espionage. The very idea of being able to non-ironically apply the word "espionage" to her daily life was thrilling to say the least.

The pay had come, just as the man promised. What was his name? She had it on a card somewhere. The money was deposited directly into her account, each payment almost a quarter of what she'd hoped to earn in a whole year. But no instructions came. For months the checks came, every two weeks. She had nothing to do and plenty of money to do it with.

She'd emailed the address the man had used a few times but got no response. Camden! That was his name. No. That wasn't a person's name. Cameron? Maybe Cameron something. He'd been average-looking, in a dark suit. Average office.

Now she checked her phone for the emails she'd sent when they'd exchanged information before, but couldn't find them in her phone. That was weird. Had she deleted them? She never deleted emails. That was the best part about emails. They never forgot.

Maybe she was fired. Maybe that's what the hangup meant. Well, she'd made a ton of money for doing almost nothing except having the shit scared out of her today. She'd find something else.

She started the car, and then felt absolutely nothing as it collapsed on itself at high speed. Metal folded, glass broke and fell, then leaped up again as if drawn gravitationally to the center into which the car was folding. The ball of material got smaller, then smaller still, and then winked out of existence entirely.

CHAPTER 9

R andolph's Jaguar was quite long and shiny, but even so, Justus took up most of the rear seating area. Janika didn't seem to mind.

"So, wait," Daniel said once inside, "we're going to Washington?"

"No," Randolph said, starting the car. "Washington is a person. He wants to show us something down at Phelps."

"Phelps the mall?"

"Naturally."

"It'll take forever to get down there at this time of day," Daniel said. It was at least ten miles away and Atlanta vehicular congestion was legendary.

"Nonsense," Randolph declared. Then he stomped on the accelerator. The big car roared like a forest fire. The size of the car combined with the ferocity with which it accelerated gave Daniel the sense of riding in a building on the crest of a continuous earthquake. He fought to control his senses, which all seemed to be shouting at his brain at the same time. Sense by sense, his brain began to untangle the mess of information.

It began interpreting information from his eyes first, which were telling him something impossible: the Jaguar was accelerating toward the side of a building at terrific speed and would certainly crash.

Next his brain decoded incoming messages from his ears which were being assaulted by the roar of the powerful engine while simultaneously being annoyed by a piercing, wavering shriek. This last sounded as though a cat were being sandpapered.

Close behind this, his mouth, larynx, and lungs reported in to say that they were responsible for the shriek, a fact about which his brain felt embarrassed but powerless. Last, but not least, his digestive organs banded together to inform his brain that they intended to forcibly eject their contents out one end or the other, possibly both.

Seconds before his organs could carry out that threat, however, and mere inches from crashing into the wall in a deadly fireball, the Jaguar turned upward and launched into the sky.

Randolph chuckled as they leveled off.

Daniel composed himself. "That wasn't very nice," he said.

Randolph nodded. "Childish, yes, I admit. But we are in a hurry. Besides, I'd expect a lighter attitude from someone dressed as you are."

Daniel looked down. Oh Jesus, no. He was still wearing the smock and tights.

There was a rumbling noise from the back seat area that Daniel took to be Justus's laugh.

"Someone's a very cheerful black bottomless abyss," Janika said.

Justus *humph*-ed.

The car was still accelerating. Daniel could see the ground below swimming by as fast as, if not faster than, he'd seen it do out of the window of a landing passenger jet. Two Canada geese regarded the vehicle with what might have been surprise, but also might just have been the dumb look those birds always wear.

They were approaching Phelps mall now, moving at a terrific speed. Daniel was afraid they were going to crash into the side of the building because of their descent angle, but the car pitched upward, slowed. It landed in front of the main entrance of Phelps mall with a light bump of all four tires. People were walking to and from the entrance but seemed to ignore the car.

Daniel got out, legs unsteady. Everyone else was already out, walking toward the entrance – even Justus, whose exit Daniel thought must have required a can opener and shoehorn.

Inside the mall, the Santa area was deserted. It looked nearly identical to the one at the mall they'd just come from, except there was no Santa, no elves, no other employees. There was a tree, a throne, a kiosk, some fake presents, some garland. No people.

"That's odd," Randolph said. He thumbed at his cell phone, then frowned, which everyone understood to mean that Washington was incommunicado.

"We should go to the coffee place," Janika said.

"I could use a coffee," Daniel agreed.

"Coffee is a vile mockery of tea, but you may do as you wish," Randolph said.

"Milk makes me gassy," Justus said.

"I think Janika's point is that if anyone knows anything about Washington not being here, the coffee place would be a likely stop. Let's have a look," Randolph said. He strode off a few paces so he could see around the Christmas tree, then pointed.

As they got close enough to see inside, Randolph's steps slowed. He spoke quickly and quietly. "Justus, on your guard please. Daniel, stay directly behind me, Janika, watch my back please.

Justus and Janika both grunted acknowledgements. Their faces became hard, like the faces Daniel had seen on airport staff who assume every passenger is literally a ticking time bomb.

They walked into the coffee shop. Two older ladies were at a table near the door, shopping bags at their feet. There was no one in line. A few people in colorful aprons milled about behind the counter, paying no attention to the customers who had just entered.

Randolph nodded to the ladies as he passed, and said, "Remember, concentrate." Daniel didn't understand this, but Justus apparently did. He grunted again, then stopped at their table.

"Ladies, I think it is time to continue shopping," he said to them in a polite voice.

"Oh, hello young man. You're quite big, aren't you?" one of the ladies said.

Justus gave a short sigh, closed his eyes, opened them again.

"Ladies, I believe you should be leaving, please,"

The ladies looked at one another, smiled, then stood up, grabbed their shopping, and walked out, chatting happily.

Justus turned and nodded at Randolph who gave a nod back. Janika looked wary, hands at her sides but fingers slightly splayed. Randolph stood in line at the cash register.

An employee walked over, a sneer on her face. "Welcome to Pequod, may I help you?" She said the words as though she would rather wade through snake-infested vomit.

"Hello," said Randolph brightly. "I'd like a tea please."

The girl huffed a laugh, threw a sneer over her shoulder at a coworker, who caught the sneer, wore it on his own face.

"Pequod is a coffee store," the girl said. "But I wouldn't

expect a dumbass mall Santa to know that." She laughed again.

The boy behind her made a laughing sound as well, but it came out sounding more like he said the sounds, "Huh. Huh," than an actual laugh. He added, "Good one, Skylar."

"I'm starting to think I should report you to your supervisor," Randolph said, sounding bemused.

"Oh yeah, old man? Well here's something you don't know: I am the supervisor!" The girl gave a shriek, then leaped over the counter at Randolph with superhuman strength, hands outstretched to clutch at his throat.

CHAPTER 10

R andolph dodged backward with surprising speed and agility. This had two immediate consequences.

First, the Pequod employee who was attempting to clutch at his throat missed with both her hands. The ferocity of the attack would have driven her and Randolph to the floor with her on top if she'd succeeded in her attempt to grab him, but as she'd missed, she was now pitching forward and would soon be sprawled on the floor.

Second, since Randolph had dodged, he was not occupying the space through which the piece of coffee making equipment thrown by the boy behind the counter was now sailing. Daniel had just enough time to recognize it as a shiny glint of metal with a black handle before it struck him on the forehead, causing an explosion of pain. He dropped like a sack of hammers.

Janika yelled, "Arschloch!" A jet of blue flame left her hands, which enveloped the attacking female Pequod employee and froze her in place.

Similarly, Randolph extended an arm with his globe in it

and declared, "Twat!" His blue flame shot out to envelop the sneering male employee, who was also frozen.

Both held the combatants frozen for a second, then Randolph said, "Right. These two must be it. Let's sit them down and have a chat with them, shall we? Justus, the door, please."

"The kid has been hit on the head with a... thing. He's down." Justus said.

"Ah. Has he? Have a look at him first then, please." Randolph was moving now, carefully maneuvering the male employee from behind the counter to sit at a nearby table. The boy's face was slack, but still had something of a sneer to it.

Janika was moving her charge as well, but with less grace. The girl toppled, fell in a heap.

"Oops," said Janika.

The girl got up, joined the boy at the table.

"All right then, tie her off," Randolph said.

Janika made a series of motions, which Randolph oversaw while keeping an eye on the boy.

"Yes, yes," he said. "Yes, indeed. Very well done."

"Thank you," said Janika. Her blue flame dissipated, but the female employee didn't seem to notice.

Randolph also made some motions, then waved the globe in front of both of the employees' faces.

As this was going on, Justus kneeled over the inert form of Daniel, thumbed first one of his closed eyelids, then the other, then said, quietly, "`khu i." One hand was clutching a gold chain at his throat, the other outstretched toward Daniel.

Daniel stirred, looked around. "Why am I on the floor?" he asked.

"You got hit with coffee thing," Justus said. He pointed.

On the ground lay what looked like a very heavy ice cream scoop.

"That must be why my head hurts," Daniel said.

"Follow my finger," Justus said, then waved it in front of Daniel's face.

"Hard not to follow a finger that big," Daniel observed, then attempted a huff of a laugh which turned into a groan of pain. He touched his forehead. It came away with blood on it. He made a strangled noise in his throat.

Justus grunted, reached out with one hand and the other on his chain, said "`khu i," slightly more forcefully this time. A tendril of light snaked out from his outstretched palm.

"OK," he said, standing. "You are healed now."

Daniel got slowly to his feet. "Wow, did you just heal me with magic?" he asked. He touched his forehead, then looked at his fingers. No blood.

Justus shrugged.

"So, wait," Daniel said. "You're a magical healer who is also a bottomless black abyss who cares about nothing?"

"Buuuegh," Justus said, with another shrug. "I am having many facets."

"We don't pick our magic," Janika said. "It picks us."

"Let's get back to these two," Randolph said. He was waving his globe again. "Right then, Skylar, to attention, please."

The female employee perked up, looked around. She blinked a few times. "Welcome to Pequod, can I help you?" she asked, again sounding as if it was the thing in life she'd least like to do.

"I wonder if you can tell us why you attacked us just now," Randolph asked.

"Oh my god, it's obvious? You're like, a bunch of assholes or something. We hate you, don't we Cody?" She didn't look at

Cody as she spoke to him, but looked over at him when he didn't reply. Cody stared blankly into the middle distance. Skylar looked at Randolph. "Why's Cody all spaced out like that?"

"He's in a magically induced trance," Randolph said. "Just as you are."

"Oh my God I'm so not," Skylar said. "Probably he's just mad at me because he's like, in love with me or whatever but I'm not intereste-" She stopped talking abruptly, then cheerfully concluded in a voice so bright it barely sounded like it came from the same person, "Hi! Welcome to Pequod, how can I help you?"

Her face twisted in horror.

Randolph smiled.

"OK, fine, I'm in a magically-induced trance. What. Ever. What do you want to know?"

"As I say, why did you attack us?" Randolph prodded.

"It's obvious? The mummy told us to," Skylar said.

"The mummy?" Janika asked.

"Yah, like, the horrible man-shaped thing that looked like swirling darkness inside, but he or it or whatever was all wrapped up in rags like a mummy. He had those gross dogs and they took the other Santa Claus away."

Randolph looked up, met eyes with Janika, Justus, Daniel. "They've got Washington, that's not good." Then back to the girl, "Right, thank you Skylar."

"Go yank yourself, you gross old man," she said, but then relaxed, her face going slack.

CHAPTER 11

"Cody, wake up please," Randolph said.

Cody started awake, said, "Huh," once, wiped at his forehead with the back of his hand.

"Why did you attack us?" Randolph asked.

"Because the dark ghoul or whatever it was told us to," he said, in a petulant but still normal teenage boy voice. His voice was all anger for the second part. "And plus fuck you guys I hate you all," Cody said, then, normal again, "Anyway I don't want to get fired."

"Why would you be fired?" Janika asked.

"I don't know, Skylar's hard to work for. She just made supervisor so she's all crazy strict, so I try to be super helpful, but now she thinks I'm in love with her or something, which is impossible because I'm gay."

"Straight people are like that," Justus observed.

"Tell me about it," Cody said.

Daniel felt an urge to look over at Justus, but also didn't want to be the kind of person who was surprised when someone let it be known, in casual conversation, that they are gay. If that even was what Justus was letting be known. He played it cool.

Randolph leaned in. "Cody, if there is anything else you think I should know, I want you to tell me, please." He was speaking deeply, slowly, and staring at Cody with great intensity.

Cody winced, turned his head, like he was hearing something he didn't like.

"Come along now, lad, let it out. You can tell me," Randolph intoned.

Cody's head was shaking now, his eyelids fluttering, but at last, he spoke in a strained voice. "You must seek the brother," he said.

"Whose brother?" Randolph asked.

Cody slowly raised an arm, as though in a trance, then pointed at Daniel.

"His," he said.

Randolph turned to look at Daniel, then turned back to Cody, nodded, then straightened. "I think we're done here," he observed. He waved his globe again. Skylar and Cody looked into it, then seemed to relax, smiled. They both stood up like they'd just finished a short break and were now going back to work.

"Can we help you?" Skylar asked, noticing Randolph. She still sounded like she didn't much want to help, but was a lot more cheerful than she had been previously. She even smiled a little.

"Thank you, no," Randolph said. "We were just leaving."

RANDOLPH TURNED AND WALKED OUT. DANIEL FOLLOWED, then looked over his shoulder to see the two employees apparently returning to their normal duties. Cody picked up the metal thing he'd thrown at Daniel, turned it over in his hand, eyed it suspiciously, shrugged, then went back behind the counter.

"What was all that about?" Daniel asked.

"You heard them. They were in thrall to a geist," said Randolph, turning to head back the way they'd come to the mall's main entrance. He was thumbing at his phone again.

"In what to a what now?" Daniel asked.

"Mind controlled by a *weihnachtsgeist*," Janika said. "It's German. The girl was right, they're a swirling black horror in human form. Sometimes they are wrapped in rags, like a mummy. They feed on fear, pain. They can control people's minds."

"And they smell bad," said Justus. "Like a rotting corpse."

"Why did that kid say I have a brother?" Daniel asked.

"Because you have a brother," Randolph said. He stopped walking. "This is, among many reasons, why I didn't want to bring you along. You see, I am about to retire. Technically, I might already be retired if HQ has processed my paperwork."

"What does that have to do with me having a brother?" Daniel asked. "I don't have a brother."

"Are you sure?" Randolph asked. "Aren't you adopted?"

"Well, sure, but." Daniel didn't know what to say or how to feel.

"We found out like this too," Janika said. "I didn't know I had a brother. He wasn't even in the same country as me. But there he is." She poked a finger into Justus's ribcage, prompting no response.

"So who is my brother?"

Randolph frowned. He looked frustrated. "Cock," he said. A small fizzle of spark and smoke rose atop his head. He sighed. "Well, I don't suppose I have a choice now but to tell you since we must go looking for him. His name is Chris Birchfield."

"Chris Birchfield?" Daniel asked, loudly.

Randolph put a hand up in a shushing motion. A passing shopper looked up from her cell phone, then back down at it. She apparently saw mall Santas and their helpers in green smocks having loud discussions all the time.

"He can't be my brother," Daniel said. "He's awful!"

"We cannot pick our family," Randolph said.

"You should see the stuff he posts on social media, though. I mean, God. None of it is overtly racist, but it's pretty clear he's a racist. Not to mention a sexist, a homophobe, plus I think he's into drugs now too. Ugh."

Randolph nodded. "I have seen it, actually. That's why I asked to be on you instead."

"On me?"

"I very much do not want to get into this. Did I mention I am about to retire?"

Daniel glared at Randolph. Janika and Justus wandered a few steps away to sit on a mall bench, respectfully out of earshot.

Randolph relented. "Yes, yes, all right. You're right of course. Forgive me," Randolph said. "I do not know who your father was, but I do know that at some point in your lives you and your brother were flagged as potential candidates for recruitment. We can do nothing until you come of age. Unfortunately, Chris got wrapped up with some unsavory elements."

"So, wait, if he's my brother, who is my..." Realization landed on Daniel. "Aunt Karen was my mother?"

"Biologically, yes," Randolph said quietly.

Daniel looked around. Shiny mall floor. Brightly lit shops. On a bench out of earshot, Justus and Janika were looking at him. Janika smiled with sad eyes.

"What about my father?" Daniel asked.

"I do not know who he is," Randolph said. "We may be

able to find out a name. Right now, though, we've been attacked, Washington is missing, and HQ has gone silent."

"Aunt Karen died a few years ago," Daniel said.

Randolph nodded, put a hand out on Daniel's shoulder. "Again, my boy, I am so sorry to be telling you this."

"It's OK, it's just, you know, super weird." He was quiet a moment. Randolph let him be quiet. Then Daniel said, "Listen I feel like I should call my Mom, but I don't have my phone. It's back in the changing room in the other mall. Can we go there?"

"Yes, I think we should do that," Randolph said. "Janika? Justus? Shall we?"

Janika and Justus stood, rejoined. As a group they began walking out of the mall.

Janika threw her arms around Daniel and squeezed him. Daniel liked that quite a lot, but then looked up toward Justus's face to see if he was about to be punched so hard that he split in half for being hugged by Janika. The giant was as impassive as ever, but Daniel thought he might have seen a nearly-imperceptible nod from the supposedly impenetrable black abyss.

CHAPTER 12

"Blast," said Randolph. They'd arrived at the entrance to the mall and could see through the large glass entrance that a uniformed mall attendant was standing by as a tow truck prepared to load up the Jaguar and take it away.

Outside, Randolph greeted the uniformed man warmly. "Hello!" he said. "Cracking day, isn't it?"

"I take it this is your car?" the attendant said. He was wearing a very businesslike expression on his face, as if he were concentrating on not letting his mouth move too much.

"Oh! Yes. Quite. I see it's in your way. I'll just move it right along if you don't mind."

"I'm afraid it's too late for that, sir. As you can see, it is being towed."

"Yes," Randolph agreed. "That does happen from time to time."

A flicker crossed the attendant's face. "How long have you been parking wherever you want?"

"Oh you know," said Randolph, waving a hand and

sounding more posh than usual. "Years and years. Have a look at this, why don't you?" He held up his snow globe.

A few minutes later, the big car rose from the parking lot, leaving the bewildered attendant behind. He was unburdened by the memory of having seen them.

"That seems like a dirty trick," Daniel observed.

"No harm no foul, as they say," said Randolph, once again thumbing at his phone.

"What's next?" Janika asked.

Randolph sighed. "A hammock? A beach? Drinks with fruit in them? Some women my age with a certain moral ambivalence?"

"Randolph," Janika said.

"Yes, yes, of course. We must find Washington. I'm still trying to check in with HQ but Declan isn't answering. In fact, no one is answering."

Daniel realized he'd been without his own cell phone for some time. He patted his pockets, remembered he didn't have any pockets, and then remembered he looked positively stupid.

"Can we go back to my mall?" he asked. "So I can change clothes and get my stuff?"

"I suppose, but if you're coming with us you'll need them," Randolph said.

"Why would I need these crazy smock and dumb tights?" Daniel asked.

"Trainee's uniform," Randolph said.

"What?!" Daniel said.

Justus rumbled. A laugh. "This I like," he said.

"Don't let them tease you," Janika said. "We're not going to make you wear that awful smock."

"What about the tights?" Daniel asked.

"Oh them? Well. They're just long underwear."

Back at the first mall, everything had returned to normal

as Randolph had said it would. Even the glass in the skylight was swept up where the broken pieces had hit the floor and replaced in its fixture overhead. How had they managed to get new glass in there that fast? Daniel guessed that magical contractors must be a lot better than normal ones.

In the changing room, he put his normal clothes back on. He picked up his cell phone, checked the screen. He'd missed a bunch of calls from his Mom. Uh oh. She'd be mad with him.

He dialed.

"Daniel! Where have you been?" She sounded flustered indeed.

"Hi mom, sorry. I'm uh, at my new job. With some work people. Doing uh, work stuff."

"Oh, I see. Have you heard from your cousin? Chris?"

He almost said, "You mean my brother Chris?" but didn't. This wasn't the time. Instead he said, "No. I don't really talk to him that much. Why, what's wrong?"

"He's missing."

"Missing? Like missing how?"

"Missing, Daniel. No one's seen him for days. I have to go. Keep your phone on you and answer my calls, please."

"OK, I will, Mom."

"Did you hear me? I said answer the phone when your Mother, who raised you and loves you more than anything, calls you."

"Yes. I will, Mom."

They said their goodbyes and Daniel hung up. Randolph was buttoning a regular suit again rather than the Santa suit, looking annoyed.

"Chris is missing," Daniel said.

"Well this is going from bad to worse," Randolph said. "Bloody well try to retire. Bloody well missing Washington, bloody silent HQ. Bloody Krampus probably on the bloody verge of destroying the entire bloody order!"

"What are we going to do about it?

"Figure it out, I suppose. Probably save the bloody world…" He sighed, snatched his hanging bag with his Santa suit off its hook. "Again."

Outside, Justus and Janika were waiting next to the Jaguar.

"The brother is missing," said Randolph.

"Who was on him?" Janika asked.

"I'm not sure," said Randolph. "I was supposed to be finished after today, you know."

"So what do we do?" Daniel said.

"I'd like to go wherever they're holding Washington and kick everyone there in the face, supposing they have a face," said Randolph. "But since we don't know where that is, we'll be off to the Birchfield residence to see if we can find your brother."

"Like Cody said," Daniel said.

"Like Cody said. Now. Into the Jag please, and we'll be off. Daniel, you know where we're going, I suppose?"

"Yeah. South Alabama," Daniel said. He climbed into the big car, this time watching to see what it took to get Justus inside, but there was no drama to it. The big man just folded himself up and got in the seat as gracefully as a dancer might. Janika too got in.

"Dear God," Randolph said, starting the car. "South Alabama. I was hoping you'd say 'the beach.'"

"No beach. There's a river, though," Daniel said.

"Ah. What's that good for?" Randolph asked.

"Snakes. Floods. Drowning yourself if you can't leave South Alabama," Daniel said.

"I am sensing that there have been many pleasant family trips," Justus said.

"Right. Well, settle in, everyone. It'll be an hour or so," Randolph said.

"An hour? It's like, a five hour drive from here." Daniel realized as he was speaking that he was sitting in a flying car.

Randolph seemed to realize that Daniel had realized he was sitting in a flying car, so he merely smiled and stomped on the accelerator. The car leaped into the sky.

CHAPTER 13

"**S**o how fast can this thing go?" Daniel asked.

"There's not a theoretical limit, but things get quite tricky when moving through the atmosphere at high speed." Randolph said.

"If we go too fast, the car will come apart," Janika said.

"Nonsense," Randolph said. "Fine British engineering, this."

"But Jaguar is owned by the Indians now," Justus said. "Tata motors."

"Bah. Still British. And anyway it's only fair," Randolph said. "We owned them for quite a long time."

"This is not something to joke about," Janika observed. "None of you have been owned before."

Randolph cleared his throat. "You're quite right," he said. "A jest in poor taste. Please accept my apologies."

Daniel wanted badly to know more about Janika's history, but sensed that this wasn't the time. Instead, he thought he might be able to help relieve the tension in the air. He said, "So, wait. You guys do or don't know who my father is? Remind me."

"We don't," Randolph said. "It might be on file at HQ, and I would very much love to go there so I could hand the rest of you off to someone else, but as they're not answering me I can't do that."

"Can't we just go there and see if anyone's around?" Daniel asked.

"We could, but HQ in this case is a plane. For security reasons, no one knows where it is at any time until we're told."

"A plane," Daniel said.

"A very big plane," Randolph said.

"Couldn't we ask the cops or Air Force or someone to help us find it so we can go to it?"

"We do have some options of that nature, but even if they knew where it was they wouldn't be able to tell us where it would be once we got to that point," Randolph said.

"I see," Daniel said. He thought he saw, but might not actually see.

"Besides. A mind-controlled teenager told us this is our priority, so, this is our priority."

Daniel thought about that for a minute. It was weird. Definitely weird. This had been a completely weird day, and it wasn't even over yet. The sun was low in the sky but had not set just yet.

"When do I get to use magic again?" Daniel asked.

"Once this is all over and we find you a proper mentor, you can get some training," Randolph said.

"That long?" Daniel asked.

"I can show you a few things," Janika said.

Randolph grunted unhappily. "There are regulations about this sort of thing," he said, but he didn't sound ready to be the person to enforce any such regulations.

"Not to worry," said Janika. "You're retiring, remember?"

Randolph grunted again. A moment passed.

Daniel thought he might have just understood that he might be learning some more magic quite soon, but didn't want to press the issue, so he let it lie for the moment.

"What can you tell us about where we're going, Daniel?" Randolph asked.

Daniel nodded. He sat up in his seat a bit. "We are going to Burton, Alabama. I don't know the coordinates or whatever so I guess we'll just have to follow the roads," Daniel said.

"That's what I do anyway," Randolph said.

"There's almost nothing there. One stop light. A gas station. A post office. Chris lives on my aunt's... I mean, I guess my birth mother's farmland."

"What does Chris do for a job?" Janika asked.

"I don't know, actually," Daniel said. "He's had lots of jobs. I don't think he's very good at keeping them."

The sun was getting closer to the horizon now. Everyone seemed lost in their own thoughts for a while. Daniel looked out the window as the sun went down. Below, the land was dark. Masses of yellow light marked cities as though someone had spilled a bucket of inexpensive stars.

He woke up with his head against the glass and an uncomfortable pinch in his neck muscles. They were descending. The Jaguar set down on a deserted two-lane highway, then began driving as a normal car would.

"Do you know where we are?" Randolph asked.

Daniel nodded. Just keep going, take the left fork when we come to the church.

"The church? Is there only one?"

"There are two, actually, but they're next door to one another."

They drove into the small town. It was just as Daniel had described it. Gas station. One stop light. But there was also a new building that Daniel didn't recognize at first.

"Hey, they got a restaurant," he observed.

Down a long tunnel of live oak trees, moss hanging from their branches, they could see the church. Randolph took the left fork, drove on. Past the volunteer fire department building, past the playground where, according to Aunt Karen, Daniel's great aunt — no, grandmother — had gone to school.

Daniel pointed for Randolph's benefit, and the big car nosed onto the dirt track that was the driveway of the Birchfield house. Bright white lights played across trees, a shaggy yard, a dark barn in the distance. The house looked like it was not only empty, but abandoned.

"Right then," Randolph said, as they rolled to a stop. "I don't quite like the look of this, so let's keep our eyes up, shall we?"

"Will do," said Janika.

Justus made a grunt that sounded like, "aye."

Daniel nodded at Randolph, who gave a wink back.

They all got out, but no one walked forward yet. They were looking around, familiarizing themselves, Daniel thought. Perhaps they were letting their eyes adjust to the darkness.

"I don't think there is anyone here," said Janika. "But-" she trailed off. "There are some woods behind the house, I think?"

Daniel nodded at her.

"Might be some animals moving around in there," she said.

They walked around the house to the left. Here they could see a parking spot with a roof over it, supported by poles, and the side of the house. Further on, they could see the back porch with its sagging screen walls and odd-angle screen door. Broken and rusted pieces of machinery lay about. Someone had purchased several broken or nearly-broken dirt bikes, partially dismantled them, then left them to rust.

Closer to the screen porch now, Daniel could see the small shack that was once a hen house, though he had no idea what was in it now. When he was a kid it had contained ancient paint cans and glass jars of nails. It probably still did. The big barn sagged, mouth open and dark, maybe 25 yards away. Beyond that, in the woods, there was a light burning. He hadn't remembered there being a light out there. Maybe there was a new neighbor who had bought some land back there.

"The back door is open," Janika said.

Daniel turned. Sure enough, he could see the crack where the back door stood slightly open. "What do we do?" he asked.

"I think we should go inside," Randolph said.

"Can't you just scan it with magic or something?" Daniel asked.

"Of course," Randolph said. "I'm a wizard."

Daniel sighed with relief. Even though he'd been in this house a hundred times, right now, with it looking so dark and sinister, he didn't want to go in.

"But we should still go inside," said Randolph.

CHAPTER 14

As much as Daniel had a sense of foreboding about going into the house, there wasn't anything horrible inside. In fact, he found something that cheered him up.

The interior of the house had changed a lot. It had always been an ancient, sagging, drafty farmhouse but now it was an ancient, sagging, drafty farmhouse that someone had attempted to turn into a bachelor pad on the cheap. Chris had gone out and gotten himself a lava lamp. A vacuum would have been a much better idea.

On the kitchen counter, though, Daniel spotted a box he recognized. He'd sent it here so Chris would send back a wrist watch Aunt Karen had given him. She'd said it had been her father's. It was nothing much to look at, certainly not worth anything, but Daniel had worn it to play dress up as a kid a few times. He'd mailed the box here in hopes Chris would put the watch in it and mail it back to him at school. Chris had gone as far as finding the watch and putting it in the box, but hadn't got around to mailing it. Daniel put it on his wrist. The expandable metal bracelet of the watch pinched his arm hairs, just like it always had.

"What's that?" Janika asked.

"My uh, grandfather's watch," Daniel said. He related the story of the box that hadn't been sent.

Janika reached out, put a finger on the face of the watch, then nodded, smiled, retracted her finger.

The rest of the rooms were empty, not only of people but of any clues as to what might have happened to Chris. Janika and Daniel flipped lights on and looked around but didn't open drawers or closets. Randolph and Justus were looking around the rest of the grounds.

As Daniel and Janika were walking back out toward the back yard, they met the other two, who wore grim faces.

"Anything inside?" Randolph asked.

"Nothing really," Janika replied. "Daniel found a watch that belongs to him."

"Did he now? May I see it?" Randolph asked.

Daniel showed the watch, on his wrist, to Randolph.

Randolph put out a finger, touched the face of the watch, then made an approving noise, retracted his finger.

"What is that?" Daniel asked. "Janika did the same thing, with the finger."

"Did she? Clever," he looked sideways at Janika. Janika made a small curtsying motion that Daniel had only seen in movies. "We put a finger on it to see if it has any magic. Here," he said. He pulled his snow globe from a pocket.

Daniel reached out as he'd seen Janika and Randolph do, put a finger on the globe. It thrummed and vibrated under his finger as though it were a ringing cell phone on silent.

"Huh," he said. "I didn't notice that before."

Randolph withdrew the globe, stowed it in a suit jacket pocket again. "It was a much more tense moment," he said.

"And speaking of tense moments, I think we're going to have to call the police."

Daniel's heart ricocheted around, bounced off his stomach. They'd found something terrible back there. Oh no. Had something bad happened to Chris? "Why?" he asked, voice strained.

"Because I believe we have found a methamphetamine laboratory," Randolph said.

"A what?" Daniel said, his voice rising in disbelief.

Justus was nodding. "Smells like cat piss. Drug making equipment. Definitely meth lab."

"Wow, I knew Chris was into smoking pot or whatever, but I didn't know he was into meth," Daniel said. "I guess pot really is a gateway drug."

Randolph shook his head. "Not really, in my experience. Often people who make poor choices make a series of them, but that's hardly marijuana's fault."

Daniel didn't know what to make of this, but realized his mouth was open, so he closed it.

"Anyway, as I say, I think we'll need to contact the local constabulary," said Randolph. "Come and have a look."

Daniel followed. As they passed the old barn, he could see that the light he'd thought might belong to a neighbor's house was in fact inside a filthy trailer home. It was parked in a clearing among the trees. Next to the trailer were two long parallel mounds of earth, as if someone had held a funeral for two limousines. Nearby was a ring of rocks, some empty beer bottles, and a few outdoor folding chairs.

Daniel went to the door of the trailer. Some concrete blocks had been stacked on the ground as a rudimentary stair. He stepped up them, nearly falling when one wobbled.

The inside of the mobile home looked like a great explanation for why no one should remember the seventies too fondly. Everything was brown or yellow, and those were the intended colors. A layer of filth helped the yellow to tend toward brown, as did the single light, which was a bare bulb in a cheap fixture overhead. In the floor was a big rectangular piece of metal on some very sturdy hinges. It was standing open. A ladder was propped up to serve as stairs to get down into the hole which the metal plate would otherwise cover. A rug was wadded up nearby.

"What's this hole?" Daniel asked.

"That would be the entrance to the drug lab," Randolph called from outside.

Janika poked her head into the mobile home, wrinkled her nose. "That's unpleasant," she said.

Daniel had noticed the smell, but hadn't really registered it fully yet until Janika mentioned it. It was like cat pee mixed with vinegar.

He carefully descended the ladder and looked around. He was in an underground chamber with two long, narrow rooms that had corrugated walls. They must be shipping containers. Some rough wooden tables were built along one wall of each room and various buckets, cardboard boxes, and discarded plastic packaging lay on them.

He made a mental note to ask Chris what the hell he was thinking when he saw him next. He had a flash then, that he might not see Chris at all. He pushed the thought from his mind.

Janika looked around with a pained expression on her face, then went back up the ladder. Daniel followed. Justus helped them both out of the hole.

"Right then," Randolph said when they were back in the clearing. He had his phone out and dialed.

CHAPTER 15

Daniel was tense, watching Randolph dial the police. He didn't think he had anything to fear from them, but the idea of standing next to a meth lab and willfully contacting the authorities unnerved him. He wanted to get away from it. Far away.

"Yes, hello," Randolph said into the phone. He gave the address, then said, "I've come looking for a friend and discovered what I believe is a drugs production facility in his backyard. I'm not sure what to do about it, but I thought the authorities should know. Yes. Very well. Thank you." He hung up.

"Now what do we do?" Janika asked.

"We wait," Randolph said.

"Why don't we just leave? We let them know it's here." Daniel asked.

"Because I want to ask them a few questions when they get here," Randolph said.

"You think they might know where Chris is?" Daniel asked.

"I don't know what they know, but in a community this

size with a ..." he searched for the right word, then landed again on "facility." "...facility like this, they might be able to help us with where we can look next."

They stood around for a few minutes. Nothing happened. No sirens. No lights.

Randolph sat in one of the folding chairs, which Daniel found peculiar given the niceness of his suit. After a few minutes more of standing, they were all sitting. Justus barely fit in his chair. The cloth of the seat creaked under his weight but held.

"About how far away would the relevant authorities be, Daniel? Do you know?" Randolph asked after a few more minutes had passed.

"A mile?" Daniel guessed. "We passed close to the local State Trooper's office on the way in. I used to play in the yard across the street sometimes. But if they're doing something more important, who knows?"

Randolph nodded.

"Perhaps a cow has stolen some milk," Justus suggested.

"Why would a cow steal milk?" Janika asked.

"Why would humans steal it from cows?" Justus asked.

"A point well made for the big man," Randolph observed.

"Hmph," Janika said. Then she gave Daniel a grin. "Hey, want to learn some magic?"

Daniel leaped out of his chair with an excited look on his face.

"I'll take that as a yes, then," Janika said. She got up too. "All right then, first things first. We all have a magical item we use to help focus. Randolph has his globe. Justus has his necklace. I have a charm bracelet." She held her arm up so that a fine bracelet glinted in the light.

Daniel wasn't sure he'd noticed it before. "OK. So what am I gonna use? Do I get a wand or something?" he asked.

"I'm not sure about a wand, but a watch perhaps," she said.

Daniel looked at his wrist. The watch ticked at him. "But this isn't a magical item, it's just my great unc- I mean my grandfather's watch," he said.

"It doesn't matter," said Janika. "It's something to which you have an emotional connection, so it can help you focus magic. It's just a tool. If you find something else later that helps better, you can switch to that."

"Let it be known that I do not condone these proceedings," Randolph intoned.

"I am ambivalent," Justus added.

Janika ignored them. "In order to use magic well, you must recognize your emotions. You must feel them. Guide them."

"How does Justus use magic if he's an uncaring black abyss?" Daniel asked.

"Because he's an abyss of bullshit." Janika said.

Justus made an unnaturally overstated smiling face.

"Terrifying," Daniel said.

Janika continued. "There are many different kinds of magic. Attack, defense, healing. Randolph is very good at attack and defense. I am learning those from him. Justus can do some rudimentary mind control and healing."

"There is also teleportation," Justus said. "But walking is faster."

"No real teleporters anymore," Randolph nodded. "I knew one, once, many years ago. Quite a practical joker."

"So what's up with the swear words?" Daniel asked.

"They're words that people tend to use when they're emotional. It's thought that they have a special resonance with magic for this reason," Janika said.

"So I just focus my energy mentally, say a swear word, and hey presto?" Daniel asked.

"Yes and no. You probably have a small affinity for a certain kind of magic. We won't know which one, if any, until we try. Here, try this: imagine a well of anger inside, welling up and shooting out, then use a word as you focus that energy out of your hand. Like so." Janika stuck her arm with the bracelet on it straight up in the air, yelled "Fich!" and a gout of flame lit the night sky, burning upward from the clearing.

"Very nice, Janika," Randolph said, sounding impressed.

"I have been practicing. Now you try, Daniel."

"Can't we get in trouble? This seems dangerous," Daniel said.

"We already called cops on ourselves," said Justus.

"Oh yeah. OK. Here goes." Daniel focused himself, like Janika said, he pointed his hand upward toward the night sky, imagined his energy going down his hand and out his fingers, then yelled "Fuck!"

To his surprise, there was a small flame, just for a second, at the end of his fingers. It reminded him of a backyard propane grill running out of gas.

"Whoa!" he said. "It worked!"

"Not bad, not bad," said Janika.

He tried a few other things. He was able to produce a small puff of cold wind at one point. A tiny tendril appeared when he tried a healing spell.

"Is perhaps good enough for healing a bruise on a small mouse," Justus said.

"Don't worry," Janika said. "Everyone's first time is like this. It's not easy."

Daniel felt a little dejected that he couldn't make a huge gout of flame like Janika or Randolph. And that his healing spell probably wouldn't even be able to cure a mouse that had been in a mouse fight. He fingered the watch on his wrist.

Just for fun, he closed his eyes, laid the fingers of his right hand on his watch, and concentrated on the church in town, with its tunnel of mossy live oak trees. He focused, whispered a word, and a sickening pulling motion rushed up his body from his feet.

He winked out of existence.

CHAPTER 16

Daniel opened his eyes just in time to find a car rushing at him. He was standing smack in the middle of the two-lane road that led through the tiny town. He jumped to his right, barely avoiding being clipped by the car's wing mirror. If the car had been taking the left fork in the road, he'd have surely been hit.

He spun around, heart feeling like it was trying to beat hard enough to push his ears off his head with sheer blood pressure. He was looking at the church now, white paint turned yellow by street lamps. To his right, the tail lamps of the car receded into the distance. To the left of the church, though, something was moving as well. He squinted to make sense of it as he stepped out of the road.

He could feel the roadway on his feet, smell the grass, feel the slightly chill air on his skin. He could smell a whiff of gasoline from the car that had nearly hit him. All this was real. Yet what he was seeing could not possibly be real.

A man with Justus's outsized muscular proportions was walking down the center of the roadway, except that this man had to be at least twenty feet tall. He had long yellow hair and appeared to be dressed in rags. Daniel could feel the roadway tremor slightly with each step the giant took. The huge form plodded deliberately out of one pool of light from a street lamp, then was picked up by another. It was dragging a ragged tree branch, as though it had either plucked it off a tree near the road or found it already broken off in a ditch.

He had to warn the others.

He closed his eyes again, concentrated, whispered. Nothing.

He calmed himself. He had to do this. He'd never outrun that thing. Whatever it was Daniel definitely didn't think it was on his side. It was just lucky he'd teleported behind it. If the thing saw him it would pluck his head off like pulling a stem off an apple.

Daniel closed his eyes again. He concentrated on his breathing. Felt the night air again. Ignored the tremors in his shoes as the huge thing stomped down the road.

He was beside the fire again. Everyone was standing, staring, eyes wide.

"What the hell did you do?" Randolph demanded, face an angry mask.

"No time," Daniel said, words a rush. "No time. Giant!"

"I can't believe he's a teleporter. I want to be a teleporter," Justus said.

"Shut up!" Daniel yelled. "There is a giant walking down the road toward us. It's like someone took Justus and used a growth ray on him or something. Twenty feet tall!"

Randolph's face went white for a minute. The way he was standing, with Janika and Justus behind, Daniel thought he might have been the only one to see the fear on Randolph's face like that, which was good, because it scared him beyond words to see a powerful wizard afraid.

"Right," Randolph said, composing himself. "They sent a thor."

"What?" Janika asked.

"They have Thor?" Daniel asked, his voice incredulous.

"No. Not Thor, just a giant who reminded someone long ago of Thor, which we now call 'a thor.'" Randolph said. "We must go. Jaguar." He put his arms out to shepherd everyone toward the car. They all ran for it, arms pumping. When they rounded the house, Daniel could see the giant in a pool of street light at the road. Justus made it to the car first, tore the rear door open, leaped inside. Janika was next. Then Randolph, then Daniel. Randolph fired the car up which responded with its customary roar.

Daniel looked out the window at the giant in the road. Its head snapped up at the sound of the car starting. It roared so loudly Daniel had no trouble hearing it over the already deafening roar of the car at wide open throttle under Randolph's foot.

The car began to rise, slowly at first, then gaining speed. As it did, Daniel saw the giant grab the base of the branch it had been dragging, lift it, and break off a piece the size of a man by crunching it down over its massive knee. The giant drew the broken off piece back and hurled it up into the sky.

"It threw a log at us!" Daniel yelled. There was no way that even a giant that size could throw that piece of wood this high in the air. It had to be six feet long, hundreds of pounds.

Randolph wrenched at the wheel and the car lurched down and to one side, an evasive maneuver. Then the log hit the rear of the car, spinning it.

"Brace!" Randolph yelled. They were going to crash.

Daniel tried to brace but he couldn't see very well. The car was spinning so fast he had no sense of where the ground was. Then it came, and the force of it was double what he'd imagined. They landed wheels down. The car gave a sickening crunch and wrenching noise and lay still. Daniel twisted to look out the back window. The giant was running toward them.

"We gotta get out!" he yelled. "Everyone out!"

Thankfully, everyone was moving. He pushed his door open and stepped out, wincing in pain. He'd done something to his ankle in the crash. The rear doors weren't opening. Randolph was out. Janika wriggled into the front seat and got out, but Justus couldn't get the rear doors open. The car had been so twisted in the crash that they couldn't come open and he was physically too big to get out of the back seat.

The giant was nearly on them now, illuminated by the car's headlights, one of which was still on despite the crash.

Randolph stepped into the light, held up his globe, roared. Daniel couldn't hear which word. A torrent of blue ice like an avalanche shot out of Randolph's hand. The giant threw up a massive arm to cover its face and eyes as the narrow cone of blizzard hit him full force. When the torrent subsided, the giant's hair and scraggly beard were frozen. The rags it wore were frozen solid on the front of its body, and the arm it had thrown up over its face appeared to be frozen solid, because it stayed in the position it was in when the magic hit, though it could apparently still move at the shoulder.

The giant clawed at itself with its other hand while screaming. Its frozen rags shattered, taking some skin with them and leaving red patches behind. When the rags were gone, the giant was nude, partially frozen, and entirely angry. Its dick and balls swung as it charged.

CHAPTER 17

J anika was frantically pulling at the rear doors of the Jaguar, trying to free Justus, who appeared to also be trying to force the doors open from inside by putting his considerable back against one side and pushing at the other with his legs.

Randolph cast a gout of flame this time, which struck the giant in the thigh. The thor seemed not to notice. It was close to Randolph now. It aimed a kick at him which landed a glancing blow, but was still hard enough to knock the old wizard tumbling away to the side.

The giant was on the car now. It could have reached across and plucked Janika off the ground, but it didn't seem to know what to attack. It was turning its head this way and that. It brought its hands down, smashed two huge fists into the hood, destroying the front of the car. The headlight went out, and the electrical system must have been damaged as well because there was now no light in the field at all.

Randolph was up again, yelling at Janika to get back. This time his gout of flame was aimed at the giant's face. It was a short burst, but enough to blind it apparently, because it began to swing wildly in all directions, roaring and clenching its teeth with rage. It ripped the hood of the car off and threw it like a frisbee hard enough to take all their heads off had they been anywhere near it.

Janika followed Randolph's lead. She backed away as he'd asked her to, but another gout of flame shot out at the giant, this time from her hands. It caught the flailing beast on the side of its head as it thrashed.

Randolph cast a thin gout of flame this time and brought it down on the middle of the Jaguar like a sword. It cut through the car like a prize bread knife through fresh rye, separating the front from the rear. The door closest to Randolph fell off, having been severed just aft of the hinges, and Justus climbed from the wreck. He bolted onto the top of the destroyed car with unbelievable speed and grace, leaped toward the giant's neck, and caught it in a hug. He then kicked one leg up toward the giant's shoulder, and used that to lever his body around so that he was sitting on the back of the giant's neck, hugging it tightly.

The giant kept thrashing, but Justus held fast, talking to it.

"Yes, yes, yes, calm down now. Calm down," Justus was saying.

Unbelievably, the giant appeared to be slowing down somewhat. It was still flailing its arms however, and one brushed the back of its neck where it found Justus. The giant clawed at him hard enough to dislodge him. Justus tumbled down the giant's front and landed on the destroyed car with a bang. The giant raised its arms again. This time if it brought those arms down it would certainly crush Justus to a pulp.

Daniel put his fingers on his watch, concentrated, whispered, then swung a fist upward with all his might. He felt the punch connect with a satisfying, meaty thump, as though he'd hit a warm leather punching bag that held two Christmas hams.

There was an ear piercing whine, a shout, then a scrambling noise. Daniel opened his eyes just in time to see Justus once again leaping up the giant's front and scrambling onto the back of its neck. The giant's hands were busy, cupping its genitals. It whimpered and cried as Justus spoke to it.

"Yes, yes, it is OK," Justus was saying to the giant. "Do not worry. Quiet now. I heal you. I am sorry my friend punched you in the balls. It will be all right."

Daniel looked up as he retracted his hands. He'd punched a giant in the nuts. He ran around the beast's legs, fearful it might decide to sit down.

"Well," said Randolph, panting and disheveled, "I hadn't seen that particular technique before, Daniel, but we'll know for next time, eh?"

"Next time?" Daniel asked, incredulously.

Janika laughed the way people sometimes do after a very stressful moment.

Randolph smiled.

Justus was still whispering sweet nothings to the giant, which was staring off into space, arms limp, apparently lost in thought.

"Wow, Randolph, your car is a mess." Daniel said. His eyes were adjusting to the darkness. The rear was smashed sideways thanks to having been knocked out of the air by a log. One side was sliced clean through and the door had fallen away. The front was smashed beyond recognition

"Yes, well. There are other cars in the world," said Randolph, wiping a hand at a patch of dirt on his jacket.

"What do we do now?" Janika asked.

"I'd like to go down to the State Trooper's office that Daniel described and ask them what the hell they're playing at," Randolph said, face grim.

Daniel laughed. "Yeah right."

Randolph raised an eyebrow.

Daniel realized he was serious. "You can't just go barging into a State Trooper's office and demand answers," he said. "They'll lock you up for sure. Whatever parts of you they don't shoot, that is."

"We shall see about that," Randolph said. "But as much as I'd like to go down there right this instant, I think we should have a rest first."

"What do we do about the giant?" Daniel asked.

"With my beloved Jag destroyed, he'll be our chief mode of transportation, I expect," Randolph said, looking up to eye the aloof giant with the smaller, whispering giant on its neck. "And our heaviest weapon. And most naked team member, until we can find him a bed sheet or tarpaulin."

Daniel couldn't believe his ears. "What? We're bringing him with us?"

"He will follow us like a puppy when Justus is done calming him down," Janika said.

"But, he just almost killed all of us!"

Janika shrugged. "They are very good at smashing things, but their minds are not complex. If you can get someone like Justus near them, you can get them to see things your way, but most of the time it's easier to just run. Less danger of smashing."

"Precisely," Randolph said. "Now, Daniel, do you think Chris would mind if we bedded down in his house for a night?"

"Probably not," Daniel said.

"Good," Randolph said. "Right. Let's do then. I'm positively knackered."

CHAPTER 18

Daniel woke up with a stiff back, having slept on the couch in the living room area. It had been a lot more comfortable when he was shorter. As he stretched, he looked around. Justus was lying flat on the floor, covered by a blanket. Janika was curled into a ball next to her brother. As a team they'd elected that Randolph, as the eldest and closest to retirement, got to sleep on the bed.

Justus opened his eyes, sat up, then got to his feet. "It is morning," he said.

Daniel nodded.

Justus walked to the nearby front door, unlocked it, opened it. Sunlight streamed into the room. Janika moaned unhappily.

"Privyet, Muromets!" Justus called out the door.

A — literally — gigantic face appeared as the giant leaned down to look at Justus. Justus nodded at the giant. The giant nodded back. Justus closed the door.

"He is ok," Justus said.

Randolph appeared at the door to the bedroom, looking a

little rumpled. He was still wearing his suit. "Did you name him Muromets?" Randolph asked.

"No," said Justus. "He does not have a name. I had to call him something. I think he likes Muromets."

"It'll do, I think," Randolph said. "Shall we go visit the Troopers?"

"Let's have breakfast first," said Janika, still balled up on the floor, her voice a croak.

"Yes, well, breakfast first obviously," agreed Randolph.

Once they'd folded blankets and walked outside, Justus motioned to Muromets, who picked the big man up and placed him on the back of his neck. Justus fought with the giant's hair for a while, but then was still. He slid around to the side so he still had a leg over the giant's neck but could see ahead.

The giant then carefully picked up Janika, Randolph, and Daniel each in turn, placing them along his left forearm, which he held against his huge body.

"Right then," said Randolph. "To the restaurant, please."

The giant began to walk. Daniel was quite worried that he'd fall off the giant's arm and then be stepped on and squished, but the giant moved smoothly for all his bulk.

They had to walk beside the road through town, around the live oak trees, because Muromets was too tall for them. Daniel saw people staring at them from the handful of cars that passed. A man in a second floor window looked up from folding clothes, saw them on the giant and said, "Holy shit!" The man stared for a moment, then shrugged and went back to folding clothes.

"So how is it nobody's called the cops to come deal with a giant walking through their town?" Daniel asked.

"They have a low-level, passive sort of magic. People see Muromets long enough to avoid him, then forget they saw him. It's only when you know for a fact that magic exists that you overcome the forgetting part," Janika said.

Muromets stopped walking. Daniel craned his neck to look toward the giant's face. Muromets whipped his enormous right arm into the air, plucked a low-flying Canada goose out of the air and then stuffed the bird, honking feverishly, into his mouth.

"Yikes," Daniel observed.

Muromets resumed walking.

"Birds also don't believe they are seeing thors," Randolph said. "So thors eat birds."

All things considered, breakfast was reasonably normal considering there was a nude giant standing outside, scanning the skies for errant fowl to pluck out of it like grapes out of a fruit basket.

As they exited the restaurant, bellies full, Randolph said, "That was appalling."

"I guess your food doesn't have to be very good if you're the only restaurant in town," Janika said.

"We could have Muromets kick the building down," Justus said.

"I don't think the food was that bad," Daniel said.

The other three blinked at him.

"All right," he said. "It's still not right to destroy the building."

"Not this building anyway," said Randolph. "Onward to the State Troopers, eh?"

Muromets loaded everyone back up, then walked across the street and down a two-lane road. A clapboard building with a plaque on it stood under a live oak. Two troopers' cruisers were parked nearby. A flagpole was near the road, with a relatively normal-sized American flag flapping in the breeze atop it and a positively gigantic white flag with a red X on it beneath.

Muromets squatted to let everyone off him, and Randolph strode confidently up the stairs of the state trooper's office with Janika and Justus close behind and Daniel bringing up the rear.

Inside they found two troopers, both sitting with their feet up on desks that faced each other. The younger one seemed startled, took his feet off the desk. The other merely turned his head.

Between the desks and the door was a counter area. Obviously they were meant to stand behind the counter and let the troopers come to them, but Randolph ignored this and walked through the open waist-high door in the counter.

"Hello, gentlemen!" he said brightly, using his posh voice.

"Sir, I'm going to have to ask you to-" the younger trooper said.

Randolph was at the desks now. He stuck a hand out to each and caught each man in his blue fire. The older trooper, who still had his feet up, put them down, sat up in his chair. The younger trooper sat up as well.

"Right then, I assume you're in charge, Sergeant Lassiter?" Randolph said to the older man.

"Ass right," Lassiter drawled.

"Did you receive a call last night about a methamphetamine laboratory?" Randolph asked.

"Ayup. The Birchfield address."

"Why didn't you come?"

"Well hell, we ain't gonna come bust a meth operation that's paying us dividends, are we?" Lassiter said.

"I see," said Randolph. "So what did you do?"

"We had to call it up to state but we let them know it wasn't a priority,"

"So no one was ever going to come out there."

"We thought about coming down there to tell whoever called us that they should get the fuck out of town, maybe rough 'em up a little if need be, but we figured the best play'd be to just see if you left on your own."

"Fair enough. Do you know where Chris Birchfield is?"

"'Course."

Randolph stared at the man, gave a percussive sigh. "Where is Chris Birchfield?"

"Down on the river at the Perkins place. Making meth or doing meth or both I reckon."

"How do we find the Perkins place?"

"Go down to the lower landing, head up river, you can't miss it."

"Why can't we miss it?"

"It'll be crawling with armed guards looking forward to shooting your head off if you come snooping around."

Randolph made a grunting noise. "We'll see about that."

He woke the troopers up with some finger wiggling, then had them look in the globe, then pocketed it and headed for the door.

Outside, Muromets was wrapped in a silky white fabric with a red X on it. He'd pulled down the flagpole, torn the state flag of Alabama off it, and was using it and the rope to clothe himself. Daniel couldn't see what had happened to the American flag. Perhaps he'd eaten it.

"Looks rather fetching, I think," said Randolph.

CHAPTER 19

Daniel knew where the landing was, and also what it was. He explained that a "landing," in this context, is a ramp that leads into the river meant to facilitate boat launches. This was done by backing a truck with a trailer attached and a boat atop the trailer into the water, then climbing into the boat and driving it to a dock. Or, if you'd forgotten to make sure your boat was still attached to your trailer, backing into the water and then watching your boat float away down river, unmanned and probably lost forever.

"Where are we going to get a boat?" Daniel asked.

Randolph looked over from his seated position on Muromets' arm, gave a slightly evil grin, and patted the giant with one hand.

Sure enough, at the landing, Muromets waded into the river and began walking upstream as if it were the most natural thing in the world. Then again, he was a giant who ate birds, so a lot of weird stuff was probably natural to him. It was slow going, but judging by the underbrush and dense trees on the banks, it was probably as fast as walking there would be.

They went around a bend in the river, then another, passing houses that faced out over the river.

"Why are the houses up on poles?" Janika asked.

"It floods here a lot" Daniel said.

After a few more bends in the river, they saw a short floating dock ahead with men standing on it, loading something into a boat. One of the men had a rifle balanced on his hip, pointed into the sky.

"This must be the place," Randolph said.

"So what do we do?" Daniel asked.

"I think we watch for a while," said Randolph.

Muromets stood near the opposite bank and held them, unperturbed by the water, which had to be cold especially since he was only wearing a stolen state flag for clothes.

The boat that was being loaded eventually pushed off the dock, started, and motored away back up stream. The men who had been loading and the one with the rifle turned to go back up toward the house. The two who had done the loading picked up rifles they'd leaned against the dock railing. Daniel had thought that at least some of these men might not be armed with high powered rifles but he'd been mistaken. Apparently they all were.

They walked up a sloping gangway to the riverbank level, then up a set of stairs to the door of the house on poles, then took up seats in rocking chairs on the porch of the house, rifles across their laps.

"Seems fairly well guarded from the front," Randolph said. Let's move around to the rear, if we can.

Justus relayed the information to Muromets, who waded across the river. The thor had to move downstream for a while until he came to a break in the cypress trees that would allow him to climb up. The break proved to be a small creek. The trees were tall and slender here, so Muromets was able to walk between them. Perhaps twenty yards up the creek, they came to a rudimentary bridge over the little stream. There were two big logs about the width of a car's tires apart, with some piece of lumber laid over them. Muromets set them down on the bridge.

"Quickly," said Randolph. "Justus, move a bit farther upstream and wait for me, please. Janika and Daniel wait with him."

Justus nodded. Muromets stepped over the bridge and splashed up the stream so anyone coming down the road was less likely to see him.

"What are you going to do?" Janika asked.

"I'm going to go and have a look," said Randolph. He turned and began walking down the dirt track in the direction of the house. As Daniel watched, he faded from sight.

"Well that's a neat trick," Daniel said.

Janika nodded, eyebrows up, then turned and picked her way along the stream, trying not to step in mud. When they rejoined Justus and Muromets, the thor was chewing something. Daniel decided not to ask what it was.

"So what was it like to teleport?" Janika asked. She'd found a log to sit on.

"I don't know how to explain it," Daniel said. "I just sort of imagine where I want to be, try to focus, and then there I am. It feels kind of like I'm being stretched out a bit, but the sensation goes away quickly."

"People who can do it are very rare," Janika observed. "When you get good at it you'll be able to bring people with you, and you might even be able to teleport short distances without an item to help focus your magic."

"Wow, really? I could rob a bank!"

"Is more trouble than it is worth," Justus said, his voice floating down from his perch atop Muromets.

There was a cracking noise behind Janika, like something heavy stepping on a stick. She leaped up, whirled, and Randolph came into view.

"There's bad news and bad news," he said.

"Let's have the bad news," said Justus.

"They have a geist. And it knows we're here," said Randolph.

Janika's face drained of color. "Oh god," she said, voice hoarse.

"Listen to me. We can do this," Randolph said, eyeing Janika intensely with a hand on her shoulder. "Anyway, we can't run from it. We're too close. You and Justus have all the experience you need and if Daniel gets into trouble he can teleport. All right?"

There were shouts in the distance. A door slammed.

"Justus, you and Muromets are up first, I'd expect. Janika and Daniel, stay out of sight but near those two."

"We are ready," the big man said from atop the even bigger man.

Muromets headed back down river again, then stepped up onto the road at the bridge. The shouts were coming closer. Randolph whirled, crashed back into the underbrush, faded from sight again. Janika gave Daniel a little push, and he began hurrying down the riverbank. They were mostly hidden by trees and underbrush, but could see that a crowd of men were advancing down the road, holding rifles bristling with lasers, scopes, flashlights.

"Shit, they have guns," Daniel said.

"Not a problem," said Janika. "We have Justus."

CHAPTER 20

The rifle guys took up positions on either side of the road, behind trees with their guns sticking out, pointed at Muromets. They shouted to one another.

"What the hell is that?"

"Holy fucking shit!"

"Is that the state flag?"

Justus had his eyes closed, concentrating, arm moving in front of him. A few seconds later, the air in front of him and the giant began to shift, as though in that one location it was a very hot day.

One of the men yelled to the others, "Light 'em up!" then started shooting. Daniel wanted to scream, but when the bullets hit the shimmering wall Justus was casting in front of Muromets the projectiles stopped then fell to the dirt in the road.

Muromets began walking faster, feet pounding the earth like falling logs.

The man farthest away dropped his rifle. He looked at his

hands as if something were wrong with them, then down at his rifle in disbelief. Then, the same thing happened to the next farthest away man, then the next. By now, Muromets was nearly upon the first man, who had emptied his magazine of bullets and not hit a single thing. The giant plucked him from the ground, gingerly took his gun away, then reached up and placed the man in the crook of a cypress tree. He did the same thing with the next two guys as Randolph swam into view behind them. He had the two rearmost men under control, having knocked their guns out of their hands and kicked them away, but the third was giving him some trouble.

The farthest man had retrieved his weapon and very nearly got the barrel up to fire at Randolph, but Muromets picked him up, took the gun away, and stowed him high in a tree like the others.

"Get me down," one of the men yelled. "I don't like heights!" He was bear-hugging the branch on which Muromets had placed him, knuckles white.

"We don't like being shot at," Randolph yelled up to him.

As if to demonstrate, Muromets looked at the gun he was holding between his thumb and forefinger, then snapped it in half.

A ball of what looked like black fire with blue edges slammed into the giant's chest, causing him to stagger backward. Muromets went down on a knee, when another fireball struck him, this time near his hips. He was thrown backward, nearly landing on Justus, who tumbled backwards in the dirt.

Justus came up on his hands and knees, then scrambled over to where Janika and Daniel were crouching.

Floating over the road ahead, was a roiling black empty space with what looked like a few ancient rags hanging from it. It had its arms spread wide, then brought them together. As it brought its hands together it gathered between them a ball of the burning power of which it appeared to be made. It flung its arms out at Randolph, releasing the ball toward him, but Randolph flung one arm up over his face and brought the snow globe up at the same time. He yelled, but Daniel couldn't tell what the yell was. The black fire broke over him like an angry sea over a rocky outcrop, but Randolph went down on one knee, coughing.

"We have to help him!" Daniel yelled.

Justus and Janika didn't waste time sitting and yelling, they ran and yelled.

Janika was casting something. A thin stream of bright yellow fire shot out of her hand at the thing hovering above the road, but the flame was diverted. It went around the geist as though affected by gravity and shot off at an angle behind the creature. She cut the spell and dodged as the geist launched a ball of fire at them. The shot went wide. Daniel felt freezing cold as it passed, as though it was not only cold but actually removed all trace of heat.

Randolph was getting to his feet now. His hair was a mess. His suit was rumpled from overwear and dirty from where he'd had to use the ground to steady himself. He spread his arms, roared, then brought them together in a clap over his head and swung downward. What looked like a hatchet made of air formed, swung, and struck the geist. The thing was knocked backward, and as it was trying to recover, the last of its rags dropped from its body. The thing fell out of the air, landing in a heap on the ground just as Justus, running the fastest, reached Randolph.

"I'm all right," Randolph said. "Stay back from it, it will burn shortly."

Daniel gasped for air, then asked "Is that thing alive?"

The twisted heap that had formerly been a whirling black mass of fire was now getting to its feet, no longer burning. It was hairless and human shaped, but where its eyes should have been there were only two smooth depressions. Its skin was a mottled ashy green, but so dark it was nearly black. Its nose was a ragged hole in its face, its mouth a sneer of pointed teeth. It made a raspy, dry hissing sound, and charged.

Justus leaped forward to meet the thing, but instead of casting a spell of some kind, he merely uncoiled his body with the grace of many hours of practice and delivered a punch to the side of the thing's face that would have taken a normal man's head clean off his neck. The geist staggered, put its hands to its head, tried to make sense of how hard it had just been struck.

"That was for Muromets," said Justus.

There was a whopping sound, and the geist shot bolt upright, then levitated just high enough off the ground so its feet, limp on the ends of its legs, brushed the dirt.

"Well," the geist's mouth said, in a deep, clear voice that seemed to be coming from all around them. "If it isn't my old friend Randolph Twisleham. How could I have forgotten about my old friend? A most embarrassing oversight."

"I am coming for you, Krampus," Randolph said.

The geist tilted its head back and laughed. It was a disgusting series of gurgles and hisses that sounded like they were destroying the thing's throat.

"Do you understand how insignificant you are? I forgot that you exist. I assume you were taken off the rolls because your pathetic human bones are too tired to bear your dusty skin any longer." It laughed again. The geist's head made a popping sound and jerked sideways at a sickening angle. "It is of no consequence. I am in complete control of your order. It is utterly wiped out. You must have noticed."

Randolph said nothing.

The geist rasped again. "Yes, I see that you have noticed. But I have a surprise yet for you old friend." The geist began laughing again. Now there were sounds of bones grinding in its neck. It collapsed in a heap on the ground, then burned. There was no flame, just a glowing line of embers that spread over the body. The thing that had been a geist was consumed, and the ash that was left behind blew on a slight breeze coming off the river.

CHAPTER 21

"**E**veryone OK?" asked Janika.

Randolph was brushing himself with his hands. "I think so. Well done during the fight, Justus. See about our tall friend, won't you?"

"Was that, thing," Daniel said, gesturing at the pile of ash, "Krampus? Is he destroyed or whatever?"

"Not quite," said Randolph gravely. "He was merely controlling that thing like a puppet so that he could taunt us."

"Hey!" one of the men up in the tree yelled. "What the fuck is going on? You gonna get us down from here?"

"We either will or will not!" Randolph yelled back. Then, to Daniel, "Let's have a look inside."

They walked down the road until the house came into view. It looked quiet.

"Not to worry," said Randolph.

Daniel worried anyway. The stairs up to the front door were needlessly creaky, just to make matters worse. There was a quality to the creaking noise that naturally exacerbated worry. When Randolph opened the door, though, no one rushed out with a gun. Inside there were cheap furnishings, bare bulbs on the ceiling. An enormous wooden spool that still had some wire wrapped around it was being used for a table. Along the wall to Daniel's right there were doors. One was slightly open, showing bunk beds inside.

Randolph went to the other, opened it, peeked in, then opened it wider. Inside, Chris Birchfield sat shirtless on a dirty couch, game controller in his hand, cigarette burning in an ashtray set on an empty beer box. He was rocking back and forth like he had to pee.

"Chris!" Daniel said. He rushed into the room.

"Hey, dickhead, what are you doing here? Huh? Hah." Chris said. "What the fuck? Who is this old guy? You're dirty as fuck old man."

Randolph said nothing.

"Chris, man I can't believe we found you. My mom's worried sick. People are looking all over for you."

"People? What people? Nah, ain't nobody looking for me," Chris said. He lit another cigarette even though one was smoking in the ash tray. He didn't seem to be able to keep his body still. His hands roved over himself, touching his head behind his ear, now his elbow, rubbing his knee.

"You've been missing for days," Daniel said.

"What? No way. I've just been hanging out with some people is all. No big deal. I'm fine. Tell your moms all is good, OK? Alright." He held the controller as if he intended to play the game, then looked around, located a beer can on the floor, tried to drink out of it, sputtered. "Shit I used that one as an ash tray." Then he laughed. Then he stared. "Shit," he said. "I meant to send you your watch."

"It's OK, I have it," Daniel said, holding up his wrist. "Listen, there's something I want to talk to you about. See, I found out-"

"Terribly sorry," said Randolph. "I must interject here."

"Sure but I was-"

"Yes," Randolph said. He quickly enveloped Chris in the blue flames. Chris stopped moving, looked a lot more peaceful.

Daniel looked at Randolph.

Randolph looked back. "He is very obviously addicted to methamphetamine," he said.

"Oh. Well... But," said Daniel.

Randolph got a faraway look in his eye, twiddled his fingers. "But there's good news. He's not a natural addict. He's been under control of the geist. Which means..."

Chris groaned, stiffening as though he had a muscle cramp in his back.

"What are you doing to him?" Daniel asked.

Chris groaned again, louder this time.

"Randolph!"

"There!" Randolph said. "Got it."

Chris relaxed, put the game controller down, sat back on the couch. The flames dissipated. "Man, I feel like shit," he said. Then he looked up at Randolph. "I don't know what you did but thank you."

"It's my pleasure," said Randolph.

"Got what?" Daniel demanded.

"Because his mind was connected to the geist, I was able to get some information. They are holding Bertram near Atlanta, in a jail," Randolph said.

"Don't tell me you're intending to break him out of jail," said Daniel.

"I think I have a better plan than you make it sound, but yes, that is, broadly, the idea," said Randolph.

"But why?"

"Because he's my friend, first of all. Because they'll probably kill him sooner rather than later. And because if he's the only active Santa, then he is Santa Claus."

"Oh," said Daniel.

Chris grunted. He'd apparently ignored the exchange between Randolph and Daniel. "Man. I never wanted to get into this nasty meth shit," said Chris. "I can't even remember yesterday, damn." He put the heel of one of his hands into his eye sockets. "Now I got a couple of assholes standing here talking about Santa Claus."

"What can you remember?" Daniel asked.

Chris shrugged. "I got in a little trouble. Lassiter pulled me over in town, said I was drunk driving. I hadn't had a drop to drink, but it didn't matter. He got his claws in me. Then I had to agree to help them move their drugs around, then I had to agree to let them put that trailer out behind the house. Whole thing snowballed. Next thing I know, well... I don't really remember what came next, actually."

There was a whining sound in the air. Daniel thought absently that a plane must be flying overhead.

Randolph left the room, strode across the floor quickly, flung the door open, looked outside. He whirled and shouted back, "We must get out! Chris, Daniel, immediately! Out out out!"

The whine was getting louder.

"Can you walk?" Daniel said.

"Hell yeah, I can walk. I'm a grown-ass man," said Chris, but when he tried to get up he was unsteady on his feet.

Daniel got underneath his arm and helped lift him toward the door.

When they reached the door and looked outside, they saw the source of the whine, which was now a roar. A huge military transport plane was bearing down on them, hanging impossibly huge in the sky.

Randolph was shouting from the porch at Janika and Justus to get as far away as they could. He got under Chris's other arm and the three of them navigated the stairs as fast as they could, then hobbled toward the road. The roar of the plane got louder, louder, and finally hammered their ears.

Daniel hobbled for all he was worth, trying to move Chris along the dirt track. Justus was sprinting toward them like a truck. He grabbed Chris, threw him over his shoulder like a sack of potatoes, and then sprinted back down the road as if Chris weighed no more than a silk scarf. Daniel and Randolph sprinted as well, much faster now that they were unburdened. As they clattered across the bridge over the stream there was a deafening boom and a wall of heat that threw Daniel into the dust. He hit the ground hard, which blew the air out of his lungs. He gasped, breathed in sand, coughed, sputtered.

To his right, Randolph, Justus and Chris were all collecting themselves too. They'd all been thrown into the dust. Ahead, Janika was running toward them. In the distance, Muromets sat in the road, one hand up to shield himself, but seemingly unsure what exactly he was meant to shield from.

"You OK? Everyone OK?" Janika was shouting. There were groans of acknowledgement that none of them were dead, but probably not, by the strictest definition, "OK."

"What'n the hell was that?" Chris asked.

"That was Krampus demonstrating that he has utterly destroyed my order and my life's work by crashing the US headquarters," said Randolph. He was looking down at his suit. He was going to need a new one, or a very good dry cleaner at the very least. "There was no one on board, by the way. At least there's that consolation," he said.

"How do you know?" Daniel asked.

"Because," Randolph said, tired eyes sad. "I am a wizard."

CHAPTER 22

They all picked themselves up, dusted themselves off. Justus had managed to return Muromets to some semblance of health, but said he needed rest. "Holy fucking shit there's a giant!" Chris said.

Daniel was about to try to explain Muromets, but realized Chris was talking about Justus.

"You're a big sumbitch aren't ya?" Chris asked, slapping Justus on the back. "Thanks for pulling my ass outta the fire back there."

"Wait 'til you see real giant," Justus said.

"What?" said Chris.

"What happened to the guys in the trees?" Daniel asked.

"We got them down. I threw their guns in the river first," Janika said. "They all headed down this road, wherever it goes."

"Can Muromets get us back down to the landing?" Randolph asked.

"I think it would be best if he carried himself only," Justus said. "But perhaps he can manage."

"We need to get out of here," said Randolph.

In the end, Muromets did manage. As the giant got to his feet, Chris said, "Christ almighty, I gotta get my life right. I don't even know what's real anymore."

Muromets ferried them across the river, slowly, on his shoulders, then placed them on the opposite bank. Boats were heading upriver from the landing to investigate the crash. Sirens could be heard in the distance.

They walked through the woods away from the river and eventually came to a barbed wire fence. A tree branch had fallen on the wire, bending it down enough to make it easy to step over. But when Chris tried to climb over it the tree proved to be rotten. It broke, and the barbed wire snapped upward, scraping against his leg.

"Sumbitch!" Chris yelled. "Damn fence nearly got my balls."

Everyone else was careful with the fence crossing.

A few moments of picking their way through the underbrush later, they emerged into a field with a road in the distance. Muromets helped them over a second fence, then they walked as a group along the road.

Daniel had a vague idea of which roads to take to get back to the Birchfield house, but Chris knew exactly where to go, having lived there all his life.

"This here's where I strung a wire across the road one time attached to a branch," Chris said at one intersection between two roads that seemed to do nothing more than bisect swathes of forest. "A truck came along and the branch slammed into it. "Scared ol' Milky Peterson so bad he pissed his overalls."

After an hour's walk along the road, they returned to the Birchfield house. They took turns showering, getting cleaned up. Muromets laid down in the barn with his legs sticking out and began to snore loudly.

"What do we do now?" Daniel asked, sitting around the kitchen table.

"We'll go after Bertie. We'll need everyone we can get to make five."

"Oh no," Janika said.

"What?" asked Daniel.

"I think I know what Randolph is planning to do. Not the five rings, surely," Janika said.

Randolph looked grave. "I'm not aware of another option," he said.

"Five rings?" asked Daniel.

"Ancient magic," said Janika.

"1945," said Randolph.

"That's pretty ancient," Janika said.

"What does the magic do?" Daniel asked.

Janika said, "It's a mutually assured destruction pact that the Santas of that era conjured up to make sure their base would never be located by Krampus or his minions. In the process, they also gave up any hope of ever finding his location. At the time it didn't matter..."

Randolph nodded. "Yes. When the magic was first created, we knew exactly where Krampus was. With that knowledge securely in hand, we gave up the ability to locate him using magic in return for being hidden from him magically as well. The only problem was..."

"The only problem was that when they got to where they 'knew' Krampus was, he wasn't there," Janika finished.

"What happened?" Daniel asked.

"You've heard the expression 'won the battle but lost the war?' Well, we won the war but didn't manage to eradicate the reason the fighting broke out to begin with."

"So, wait, you're telling me another world war is coming?" Daniel asked.

"Absolutely. There is nothing Krampus loves more than war," Janika said.

"I'm not so sure," said Randolph. "I couldn't tell you why, and war certainly does fit his modus operandi to foster destruction, but, something is different. I can't put my finger on it exactly yet."

"We do not have five Santas," said Justus.

"We are close. Bertram is one, I'm two, and I think you two are ready to move up. That makes four."

"What about the fifth?" Justus asked.

"Leave that to me," said Randolph. "First things first. We need rest, then we need to get back to Atlanta and break our man out of jail."

CHAPTER 23

Daniel woke up with a crick in his neck, this time because he had slept on the floor. There was a rumbling noise outside. Going by the noise, someone was driving up to the house. He leaped to his feet, then ran to the nearest window, banging his hip on a door frame as he went by and nearly falling down. He used his fingers to spread the blinds apart and saw an ancient pickup truck rolling up the dirt track toward the house. He was about to yell to everyone to wake up but then realized it was Randolph at the wheel.

Randolph drove around to the back of the house, and Daniel heard the old farm truck shut off as he was walking out the back door.

"What's this?" he asked as Randolph was getting out.

"This is a farm truck," said Randolph. "I've just bought it from a gentleman down the road. He's told me it's got something called a Windsor in it."

"What does that mean?"

"I haven't the foggiest," said Randolph. "But I assume it is named after my queen, and is thus of highest quality."

"How is everyone going to fit in the truck?" Daniel imagined riding in the bed of the truck all the way back to Atlanta and shivered. Even in the South's mild winters, it would be a cold proposition to go that far in the open air.

"Not to worry," said Randolph. "We are going to leave Muromets here for the time being."

Randolph roused Justus, and the two of them coaxed Muromets out of the barn. The thor had apparently had a very restful night's sleep. He seemed spry and pleased to see everyone. Bits of hay clung to his long hair and beard.

"Murr," he said. It seemed like a happy sound.

Justus and Muromets headed across the road and returned with the smashed bits of Randolph's car, which had apparently lain in the field there undisturbed. Daniel thought perhaps Randolph had put some sort of protection spell on it.

Randolph eyed the smashed remnants critically. "I shall miss that car quite a lot," he said.

He began to hover over it, looking at twisted car parts, whispering to them, touching them. Daniel thought at first that he was going to try to repair the car magically, but it didn't appear to be so. The parts didn't seem to change, at least not visibly. After going around the car and touching much of it as if he were somehow apologizing to the car with his hands, Randolph stood near the two halves of the broken Jaguar and waved his arms as though he were conducting a symphony and the two halves of the Jaguar were each musicians.

"Bloody fuck," he said, raising one hand as though drawing sound from the string section. "God damn," he pronounced, raising the other hand. Tendrils of heat haze began to appear, reaching toward Randolph like shimmering tentacles, then swirling around his hands. He continued to swear, and the energy began to glow white hot around his hands as though they'd turned into miniature suns. He looked a bit like a very old, very well dressed, male cheerleader.

Daniel did not make this observation out loud.

At the height of the incantations, Randolph whirled, emitted a final, "Cock!" and pushed his hands, palm out at the farm truck, which rocked on its ancient springs with creaks and rattles as it accepted the energy. Daniel thought a piece of the old thing might fall off, but nothing did.

"There we are," said Randolph. "Perhaps we should call her the Flying Windsor."

"You want us to fly in that?" Janika asked.

"Yes," said Randolph. "The Flying Windsor indeed, I think."

They said their goodbyes to Chris, thanked him for welcoming them overnight.

"Guess I'm gonna have to go to some kinda fuckin' rehab or something," he said. "I'm not trying to be a meth head all my life. I like teeth."

"You could hang out with my parents," Daniel said. "They'll take care of you."

"Nah," said Chris. "I'll be alright. What're y'all gonna do about that big fucker?" He nodded his head at Muromets.

"Well, it's a bit of a problem at the moment," Randolph said. "I presume he had been mooching about the woods behind the house where you were imprisoned?"

"Honestly, I don't remember," Chris said. "But that could be. Lotta woods back there."

"Would you mind terribly if we left him here for the time being? He won't be any trouble, unless you're particularly partial to birds. And he'll be a very effective security system."

"Only thing I'm worried about is Lassiter getting it in his head to come fuck with me some more," Chris said.

"Justus, can you ask Muromets to help guard the property?" Randolph asked.

Justus nodded.

"If you need to go somewhere, just ask Muromets to join you. It means walking, and people will act very surprised, but after you're gone there should be no lasting repercussions," Randolph said.

"Think he'd help me bury all that meth lab shit for good?" Chris asked.

"I will ask him," Justus said.

"Good enough," said Chris.

Randolph, Janika, and Daniel crammed into the cab of the truck with Justus in the bed. Justus volunteered for the bed of the truck, which was fortunate because he'd barely have left room for a driver if he was inside the cab.

To Daniel's surprise, the truck lifted off the ground just ask the Jaguar had, and began heading for Atlanta, this time traveling more as the crow flies since Randolph had a better idea of which direction he was going.

৩১৫

WHEN THE TRUCK'S TIRES BUMPED ONTO A SIDE STREET AND they began driving as normal, Daniel was glad to be back in a city. Randolph pulled the truck up next to the valet's podium at one of the nicer hotels in town.

"How can we afford to stay here?" Daniel asked.

"I'm not sure we can," said Randolph. "But if our order truly has been wiped out, then no one's going to be checking the credit card bill, are they?"

"So, if the card works at all, we get a nice room. If not, we're homeless?" Janika trailed off.

"Then we all get to stay in my dorm room," said Daniel.

"Let's hope the card works," said Randolph.

They all looked extremely rumpled, but the hotel's staff did not comment or raise an eyebrow. In fact, once Randolph produced the black credit card he carried and the staff verified that it did indeed work, the staff swept the group through the hotel with some measure of deference. Randolph invited everyone they interacted with to have a look into his snow globe. They went away looking dreamy.

Inside the room, Daniel was amazed. "I've never been in a house this nice, let alone a hotel room. Can't believe you guys are staying here."

"Would you like to forget you've ever seen a hotel room this nice?" Randolph asked, twirling his globe.

CHAPTER 24

"Why did you make all those people forget they saw us?" Daniel asked.

"Because our order is obviously compromised at the highest levels. They'd know exactly where we are and what we're doing. It would be bad to be attacked yet again," Randolph said.

"But not the worst thing?" Janika asked, sensing Randolph was leaving something out.

He sighed. "In a way it would be even worse to not be attacked. That would mean that Krampus believes his plan to be too far gone for us to matter. I fear that's where we are." He paused to let that sink in. "But we can't let that worry us. We have a jailbreak to plan."

There were many facets to the planning of the jailbreak, as it turned out. Randolph made some calls to a men's clothier he knew about near the hotel. Randolph then suggested that he, Janika and Justus walk over to the mall to get some new clothes for Janika and Justus.

"Can we go by my dorm room as well?" Daniel asked.

Randolph raised his eyebrows. "Why don't you go there yourself? You're a teleporter, aren't you?"

"Can I go that far?" he asked.

"We'll never know until you try," Randolph said.

Daniel closed his eyes, stood in the middle of the room, imagined himself standing in his dorm room. He focused, tried to remain relaxed, and whispered, "Balls." He felt confident that he'd be able to do it, somehow, so he tried to focus on what the sensation felt like as he was transported. It felt sort of like there was a ripple in the fabric of everything. He'd heard the term spacetime used to describe everything, so he figured he might as well use that term too. It felt like someone grabbed spacetime and snapped a wave into it, like someone might do when making a bed. The wave rolled up from his feet, to the top of his body. When he opened his eyes, he was in his dorm room.

"Haha!" He laughed out loud. He punched the air a few times in triumph, then gathered a few toiletries and some clean clothes. He should probably let the others know it worked, though.

He concentrated again, and imagined himself back in the hotel room. The wave rolled up his body. He opened his eyes.

He was standing in the hotel again. He opened his eyes. This looked like the right room, but he was standing next to a couch, on which was a nude older woman with grey and blonde hair, apparently asleep. She was positively gorgeous, certainly a devastating beauty in her young life, now a master-piece of the mature female form.

Daniel nearly yelled in surprise, but shut his mouth and clamped a hand over it. Shit! Something had gone wrong. He'd gotten the floor number wrong, or something.

He closed his eyes again, felt the watch on his wrist, concentrated, whispered, opened his eyes.

A very beautiful older woman, nude on a couch. Her eyes

fluttered open. She swiped the back of a finely boned hand across her face, said, "What's that dear?" then opened her eyes, saw Daniel standing there, and screamed.

"I'm sorry!" He yelled, and ran for the door.

A couch cushion nearly missed his head.

"Security!" the lady yelled.

Daniel didn't turn to look. He yanked the door open and ran for the end of the hallway and the stairs. Going by the numbers on the other doors in the hallway he'd somehow ended up two floors too low. Hadn't he? Or maybe he'd remembered the correct floor number wrong. His instincts proved partly right. He found the correct room two floors up. Randolph answered the door.

"I need your help," Daniel said. "Right now."

They managed to make it back downstairs in time to intercept the hotel staff on their way to respond to the woman's calls for security. Randolph, using the globe, convinced them that all was well, then went to the lady's door and put on his posh voice.

"Concierge, ma'am," he said to the door. "May I help you?"

"A man was in my room!" she said from the opposite side of the door.

"Not to worry, I have him right here," said Randolph. He reached out and hooked an arm around Daniel. "I'm just about to hand him over to the police. Can you confirm that this is the criminal?"

The woman opened the door angrily, stared at them both. She had put a robe on. "That's the pervert," she said, pointing at Daniel. Then she asked Randolph, "Why are you so rumpled looking?"

"My apologies, ma'am," said Randolph. "It was a bit of a scuffle to catch this degenerate." He gave Daniel a shake.

"Now if you'll just have a look into this," he said, raising the snow globe.

On the way back up to the correct hotel room, Randolph asked, "I take it you forgot our room number?"

"I don't think I did," said Daniel. "But maybe."

"I'm afraid I'm not much help in teleportation," Randolph said. "But there is likely to be danger of inaccuracy unless you are well rested, focused, that sort of thing. We cannot cast powerful spells indefinitely any more than we can run indefinitely."

"Yeah, that makes sense,"

"Having said that, I do admire your taste in women. She was quite a specimen."

"I didn't mean to see her naked," Daniel said. "I feel awful about it, invading her privacy like that."

"Not to worry. She won't remember."

"What happened?" Janika asked, when they returned to the room.

"Daniel's had a teleportation mishap, seen a beautiful woman naked, and now he's quite flustered," Randolph explained.

"That's a quite childish use of your powers," Janika said, face dark.

"How naked?" Justus asked.

"Entirely," said Randolph.

"Justus!" said Janika.

Justus shrugged.

"Randolph!" said Daniel.

Randolph grinned. "All right," he said. "I said it was a mishap. Our Daniel's not a pervert, he just teleported incorrectly. Anyway, it's all smoothed over now. And he's gained some idea of how far and how fast he can transport himself."

Daniel wanted to say something reassuring like "I would never try to see you naked," for Janika's benefit, but wasn't able to form the words on his lips since they were spiritually, if not factually, lies.

"Mistakes happen, I suppose," said Janika.

"I feel terrible about it," said Daniel. "Even worse than I feel about seeing Muromets' gross dick and balls."

"Let's all get cleaned up and rest a bit," said Randolph. "We have a jailbreak to plan."

CHAPTER 25

This time, Daniel was more careful with his teleportation. He didn't try to go the few miles from the hotel room to his dorm room and then immediately back. He changed, showered, made sure he felt rested, and then teleported back without issue.

"Right," said Randolph, after Daniel opened his eyes. "Any more nudity?"

"Thankfully, no," said Daniel.

Everyone looked at least a little refreshed. Justus was still showering. Daniel wondered how he'd managed to wedge himself into a hotel shower, but then, this was a pretty nice room. It might have lots of shower space.

Randolph was in a new herringbone tweed suit, looking much less rumpled. He seemed very pleased to be cleaned up. "You know," he said. "You should try teleporting with someone else. I'm sure it would cut your distance down quite a lot, but if you could develop it, it would be quite a worthwhile skill."

"And you should try without your focusing item," said Janika. "That will help too."

"I don't want to risk teleporting you into that lady's room, Randolph," Daniel said.

"Pity," said Randolph.

Justus emerged, scrubbed and dressed. "I am ready for crime," he said.

"So say we all," Randolph said.

"What's the plan?" Janika asked.

Randolph said, "I think we'll split into two teams. You two, Janika and Justus, will create a diversion, Daniel and I will find and extract Bertram, relying on Daniel to help with things like going around locked doors and opening them from the other side. I should be able to figure out what part of the building he's in if I can get close."

"I think we should try something a little easier," said Janika.

"Like what?" Randolph asked.

"Fly in in the truck, figure out where Bertram's room is, cut a hole in the wall, get him out."

"Hm," said Randolph.

"Why don't we just use your globe to walk right in the front door?" Daniel asked. "We could find out exactly where he is then make everyone forget we were there."

"I like it, but I think it might get out of hand." said Randolph. "Janika and I can manage a few people at a time, but if a couple of guards came around a corner suddenly it would be a problem. I think our best bet is to land the truck on the roof, find our man, fly away into the night."

"Good enough for me," said Janika.

"I have never broken into a jail," said Justus.

Janika looked at him. His face was his face, showed nothing.

"Yes, well, in any case I think we have a few hours until it's properly dark enough for such a caper," said Randolph.

"In the meantime, Daniel, why don't you work on fine tuning your teleporting skills?"

"I thought you didn't condone those proceedings," Daniel said.

"That was before I knew you were a teleporter, my boy," he said. "Now, why don't you tell me the steps you are going through to focus your energy?"

Over the next couple of hours, as the sun went down, Randolph tried to help Daniel improve his teleporting skills. Not being a teleporter himself, Randolph couldn't help as much as he could help with burning, frost, or simple mind control spells, but he did know a few techniques he'd read about somewhere.

By the time night had fallen, Daniel could teleport with another person from one room to another, he could make a jet of flame come out of his hand that would certainly deeply annoy someone (if not directly injure them), and he even, once, teleported himself without his watch from one couch cushion nearly to the next one.

"Not bad at all," said Randolph. "You'll be quite a Santa in your day, I expect."

"When will that be?" Daniel asked.

"Unless we manage to thwart whatever Krampus has planned, never." Randolph said, with incongruous brightness. "But it won't matter because we'll all be dead." Then, after a moment's thought he added, "Burned to radioactive ash, I'd expect." After yet another moment he added, "I could use a drink."

Instead of a drink, Randolph got to his feet. They all piled into the truck after the valet brought it out, drove around to a darkened alleyway and rose into the air. The truck's aging suspension creaked with relief as its weight plus that of four people rose.

They followed city streets toward the east side of town,

where the maps application on Daniel's phone said the county jail was. When it came into view, it proved to be four seven-sided buildings arranged in a shallow semicircle. They hovered nearby and regarded the building, lit up from the ground by powerful lights.

"You see?" Janika said. "If we tried to go in a hole in the side we would be seen. Powerful lights"

Randolph nodded. "You are quite right."

The truck floated higher and closer. It didn't look like there were any guards around, which was good. They decided to descend to the roof, then Randolph would do his best to search around for Washington magically.

"Can't you turn the engine off?" Daniel asked.

"What, and fall from the sky?" said Randolph.

"The exhaust is pretty loud. Someone will hear," Daniel said.

"It's over fifty years old. Your exhaust will be as loud when you're that old, believe me,"

They were close now, almost touching the closest building. Finally the tires touched down and Randolph turned the motor off.

There was a sickening movement, just as Randolph was closing his eyes to have a look around for Washington. Then there was a cracking noise and the truck lurched to one side.

Justus leaped out of the truck bed the other way, looked underneath the truck, then hissed, "broken through!"

"Shit," said Randolph. A flashbulb of power snapped over his head. He scrambled to get out his driver door. Sure enough, the weight of the truck's tires had destroyed the roof of the building. They hadn't broken all the way through, but the impressions in the roof were certainly deep enough that anyone below would have heard, and that's if they hadn't been hit on the head by falling concrete.

Someone was shouting. An alarm began to go off.

"Damn and blast!" yelled Randolph. Then he was oddly quiet, searching for Washington. His eyes popped open as more shouts could be heard below.

"I've got him, I think. But there's bad news. He's in a deprivation tank and he's in the other building."

"A deprivation tank?" Daniel asked.

"No time, no time," Randolph said, shaking his head. "Back in the truck. Justus, you drive."

Justus leaped into the driver's seat, Randolph into the bed of the truck. Justus took up most of the cab, and Daniel was shoved against Janika's body. He was very, very aware that his arm was resting against one of her breasts.

The truck began to lift again, with Randolph yelling instructions to Justus about where to drive it. They moved over to one of the far buildings, then, still floating in the air, Justus backed the truck up to the wall of the building with a bang.

Below, Daniel could see the flashing lights of officer's cars, which he found odd. Why had they needed to turn their lights on when they hadn't driven anywhere? He guessed it must be instinct.

In the bed of the truck, Randolph was standing now, waving his arms. He yelled, "Motherfucker!" and spread his hands apart. Between his spreading hands was a bolt of white-hot fire that thinned in the middle like taffy. When it broke, Randolph whipped the white-hot energy which stuck to either hand at the wall of the jail. It scored and cut the concrete outer surface wherever it hit. He began to strike again and again at the brick. Pieces fell away below.

Soon, Daniel could see into the room beyond. The hole wasn't nearly big enough to walk through, but he could see industrial green paint on block walls lit by fluorescent light. There was a black cylinder inside that had to be the tank. It was big enough to put a man inside, and it had all manner of tubes and wires running to it.

"Daniel!" Randolph yelled. "Get in there and start unplugging!"

There was a popping noise that Daniel didn't understand, followed by what sounded like someone throwing a handful of rocks into a car hood.

"What was that?" Daniel asked, knowing the answer, horrified by it.

"I think was shotgun round. We are out of effective range," said Justus.

"Daniel could you get in the fucking jail and unplug the fucking deprivation tank right fucking now, please?" Randolph yelled. The white hot fire he was wielding sparked and popped as he swore. On the last "fucking," a finger-thick arc of electricity shot between Randolph's hands.

Daniel closed his eyes, concentrated, popped out of existence.

He was in the room now. He looked out the window and was looking out onto a central room with a desk area. A man there was speaking excitedly into a radio. The man looked up, locked eyes with Daniel through the glass set into the cell door. The man dropped his radio and began to scramble to get to the cell Daniel was in.

Daniel opened the tank. A grey haired black gentleman floated in the water like a statue that had tipped into a swimming pool. There were all manner of electrodes attached to the man's body, which Daniel began to disconnect. He heard the guard hit the door to the cell, heard the jingle of keys.

Without thinking, Daniel leaped into the tank with a splash, wrapped his arms and legs around the man inside, and focused with all his energy on the bed of the truck. He whispered.

There was a rolling sensation, then a wet squish as he and Bertram Washington landed in a tangle in the bed of the truck. There were lots of clanking noises now as the policemen on the ground fired pistols and shotguns at the truck.

"Go!" screamed Randolph. He dove on top of Daniel and Washington. Justus hit the gas and the old truck's loud exhaust stumbled, caught, roared. They streaked away into the night.

CHAPTER 26

R andolph was laughing his head off, sat with his back against the cab of the truck.

"That has to be," he said, tears streaming from his eyes, "The worst jailbreak I have ever seen. And we are wizards! Bloody wizards!"

Daniel extricated himself from his bear hug of the sopping wet gentleman in the truck bed. Bertram Washington was stirring.

"Where am I?" Washington asked.

Randolph was composing himself, wiping his eyes.

"We just broke you out of jail, sir," Daniel said. "They had you in some kind of tank or something."

"Well that explains why I'm wet, but why am I in my underpants, and why were you hugging me?"

"I had to grab you and teleport you out of the room, sir. A guard was coming."

Bertram Washington's eyes got very wide. "Oh my God," he said, voice full of wonder. "I'm freezing my balls off."

EVERYONE AGREED THAT THE FARM TRUCK HAD TO GO. Randolph was saddened by that realization, but eventually acquiesced. Too many people at the jail had seen it, and besides, it was shot full of holes. Some of them were down to the gunfire. Some had been in the truck's body when Randolph bought it.

They decided to leave it on the roof of the hotel for the time being. Even though they'd already had trouble with parking the truck on a roof, they thought that the hotel, being a newer building, might be stronger. Just to be safe, Randolph hovered the truck a few inches above actually touching down on the roof and everyone got out to lighten the load.

"I have an idea," said Daniel. "Why don't I just drive it somewhere secluded, park it, and teleport back?"

Randolph looked at Washington. "What do you think, old boy?"

"I think," said Washington, shivering and hugging himself. Then he yelled, "That I am cold!"

"Oh!" said Randolph. "Yes, of course."

He threw an arm around Washington, then shepherded him toward the door down into the stairwell. There was an audible alarm on the door, but it only managed to make a single electronic woop before Randolph silenced it with a finger twiddle.

"Wait," said Daniel, "How do I drive the truck?"

"Don't worry," said Randolph over his shoulder, "It will do what you want it to do. Just don't think about falling out of the sky."

The door closed.

"I'll come with you," said Janika.

Justus didn't say anything but hopped back into the bed of the truck.

"I don't think I can teleport with all three of us," Daniel said.

"Don't worry, we use ancient magic," said Justus, settling into the truck bed with his back against the cab. "We'll take the bus."

Daniel had a few thoughts about the quality of the ancient magic represented by Atlanta's city buses, but kept them to himself, not wanting to represent his city badly to visitors.

Piloting a flying car proved to be less difficult than Daniel might have guessed. It really did go where he wanted it to. He'd assumed Randolph was pulling his leg about accidentally thinking about falling, and that instinct proved to be right as well. The truck seemed to have safety features, for lack of a better word, in that it wouldn't just plummet out of the sky unless you wanted it to. They hovered over the city lights, looking for a darkened parking lot in which to abandon the truck.

"So," Daniel said. "How are you?" As soon as he said it, he felt like an asshole. It felt like a pretty lame question to ask.

"Not bad, considering," said Janika. "It has been an exciting couple of days."

"Is it always like this? Hanging out with Randolph?"

"We have only been with him a couple of weeks. It's like he says, he was all set to retire, but was asked to stay on. They asked him to try to mind us a bit, then to mind you as well. Same thing."

"Where did he find you?"

"I was held by some very bad people," she said. "It is not very nice to talk about."

"Oh, sorry."

"No problem. Perhaps someday I will tell you."

"What about Justus?"

"Also not very nice," she said, with a small smile.

"Yes," came the muffled voice of Justus from the other side of the cab wall. "Was not very nice."

Daniel spotted a darkened parking lot downtown. He wouldn't normally have gone walking about this area of town at this hour of the night, but with a couple of wizards for company he thought it might not be so bad. If they walked a few miles north on Peachtree they'd be in Midtown and could catch a cab easily there.

The lot was very dark indeed, and there was a trash dumpster to block the clear view of the truck from the street. If they leaned some of the discarded shipping pallets that were lying near the dumpster against the rear of the truck, there's no telling how long it would be before someone spotted it.

They all got out, leaned the pallets against the truck. Justus dragged a fallen tree limb over and laid that against the bed of the truck as well. The old farm vehicle would probably rust away into nothing here and never be found.

Just to be safe, Justus ripped the license plate off.

"We could have found a screwdriver or something," Daniel said.

"Is only aluminum. Tears easily. Besides, screws are rusted," Justus said.

"What are you going to do with it now?" Janika asked.

Justus shrugged. "Dispose of it somewhere far from the truck."

He tried sticking the plate into a rear jeans pocket but it was too wide, so he stuck it down the back of his pants. He didn't want to be seen walking down the street with it in his hand.

The parking lot was fenced in. Janika could cut a hole big enough for them to wriggle through using a fire spell, but it would have to be a pretty big hole for Justus to get through, and the hole would probably make someone want to look around the lot, which would mean they'd locate the truck.

Instead, Daniel got some teleporting practice in. They chose the darkest corner of the lot, then Daniel had Janika stand close to the fence. He concentrated, and was able to teleport himself, with her, onto the other side.

Then he teleported back, and tried the same trick with Justus. It worked. Mostly. An edge of Justus's shirt snagged on a piece of the fence and had to be ripped free. They began walking north, heading in the general direction of Midtown. The streets were on a grid, so it was easy enough to find their way, but this wasn't the nicest part of town.

As they passed a man sitting slumped in the sidewalk, Daniel could swear the guy had one eye open, but closed it when he realized Daniel was looking. Perhaps he was imagining things.

They walked on.

Daniel tried to forget about it, but eventually couldn't resist saying something.

"Do you guys feel weird?" he asked.

"No," said Justus. "But we are being followed."

"What?" Daniel hissed. "Who is following us?"

"I don't know," said Justus. "But perhaps they will want to fight."

"Should we run?" Daniel asked.

"Then we would miss the fight," said Justus.

CHAPTER 27

"Hey, what are you kids doing down a street like this one?" a voice asked. A thin man in a hooded jacket had stepped out of a doorway ahead and walking down the sidewalk toward them, another man behind. Both were wearing what looked like army surplus clothes, except for Hoodie's hoodie. The one in the rear was meaty looking, but pudgy.

"Would you like to attempt to rob us?" Justus said, loudly.

"Justus," said Janika.

Hoodie guy whistled, then coughed. Two more scruffy-looking people stepped out of an alleyway behind Justus, Janika, and Daniel.

"Gentlemen, we mean you no harm," said Janika.

"I mean them harm," whispered Justus. Daniel had never heard him whisper before. It was weird to hear a small sound coming out of a guy that big.

"My brother is very big, and a very good fighter. He's actually sort of looking forward to punching you. Let us move along, and we can all have a good night," Janika said.

"Why don't you shut your mouth, bitch?" said Hoodie

man. He reached into his hoodie pocket and withdrew something shiny. Daniel couldn't see what the man held clearly, but his brain yelled, "Gun!" Hoodie man pointed it at the ground, but the threat was clear.

Janika sighed.

Justus grinned. Then, he took three quick steps backward and drove an elbow into the guts of one of the men approaching from behind. He did this without ever looking backward to see where the men were, exactly. The other got a fist in the face. Both went down.

Daniel was in awe of Justus's movements. He'd seen fights before but this was something else. It was like Justus was the world's most talented dancer, only his dance moves hurt people.

"Stop!" yelled Hoodie man, "Or I'll shoot this bitch!"

He pointed the gun at Janika. Daniel jumped, shoved Janika to the side. They fell between two parked cars. Daniel whipped his head around in time to see Justus fly by the gap between the two parked cars, arms outstretched. Then there was a grunt, and someone said, "unf!"

Daniel and Janika got up. Justus was standing over the pudgy guy, who was collapsing to the sidewalk and holding his head. Justus was turning something over in his hands. Hoodie man was sitting down against a building, holding his chest and wheezing.

"Ow, that hurt," Hoodie man said.

"You threatened to shoot my sister," said Justus, not looking at him.

"Well, I wasn't gonna do it," said Hoodie man. He rubbed at himself and winced. "That's not even a real gun."

"Yes," said Justus nodding at Hoodie. "This is always how it is with people like you. They do asshole things, and then when they get what they deserve, they try to make it someone else's fault or explain it away."

Justus stepped over Hoodie man's outstretched legs, walked over to Daniel and Janika. He held out the "gun," which was a piece of pipe that had been taped to a piece of wood. In the dark, it looked menacing enough. It had certainly fooled Daniel.

Daniel could see out of the corner of his eye that Hoodie man was fumbling with his jacket. Before Daniel could look to see what he was doing, the scruffy man lunged at Justus, swinging an arm over his head. Whatever was in his hands glinted in the street light. "...Let's see whose fault this is!" he was yelling. There was a metallic sound.

Justus had whirled by this time and backhanded Hoodie man across the face. Hoodie man went down again, and something clattered out of his hand. It was a steak knife, like you would find in a low end steakhouse. It wasn't much by knife standards, but still would certainly have been good enough to stab Justus in the small of his back had he not had the license plate he'd ripped off a flying farm truck tucked there.

Hoodie man looked up at Justus with wonder, horror. "You're a robot!" he said. "I knew it! I knew the robots would come."

"Beep boop, motherfucker," said Justus.

Hoodie man screamed in terror, scrambled backward, then got to his feet and ran around a corner.

Justus looked at his fist, turned it this way and that, then, apparently satisfied, he put his arm down.

"We should get a sandwich," he said. "I am hungry."

"Where did you learn to fight like that?" Daniel asked.

Justus shrugged. "Where I come from, my only value was as a fighter. So I became a good fighter."

"Can you teach me?" Daniel asked.

"No," said Justus. He turned and walked away down the sidewalk.

"Well that answers that," Daniel said.

"Remember," said Janika. "Not nice places."

Daniel did remember.

"Mmmuhg," moaned a man lying on the sidewalk. "Did a car hit me?"

"No. More like a tank," said Daniel.

Janika and Daniel followed after Justus, giving him a half a block worth of space, then sped up and caught him. He was as quiet and grave-looking as usual, which Daniel took as a good sign.

The lights of Peachtree Street were ahead. They were still not in a great part of town, but at least they weren't on darkened side streets anymore.

"That's the Olympia building ahead," said Daniel. "With the big lit up soda sign on top."

"Do they sell sandwiches?" Justus asked.

"No," said Daniel.

"Bah."

CHAPTER 28

"That can't actually be your plan," said Bertram Washington. He was sitting in the hotel room in a fluffy white bath robe.

"Why not?" Randolph asked.

"Because it's a terrible plan. You'll bring about the end of our entire order, not to mention alert Krampus to the location of the-" Washington paused and whipped his head around the room. "Are all these people OK?" he asked.

"They are our team, yes," said Randolph, "But they haven't yet become Santas."

"Then they're not OK!" Bertram said.

"Sir, I don't think you appreciate the gravity of our situation," said Janika. "As far as we know, we are the entirety of the operating Santas in the US if not worldwide. Well, Randolph and you are."

"Wh," Washington said. "But that w-"

Randolph nodded. "Which would mean, since you outrank me, that you are our Santa Claus."

"Well in that case I officially decree that this is a shit plan," said Washington. He jerked his hand downward twice to emphasize the shitty-ness of the plan, but didn't really need to, given that a deep purple aurora of energy flickered at the peak of his head as he swore.

"How long would you like us to wait to come up with something superior, sir?" asked Randolph, speaking in what Daniel thought was one of those very compliant tones of voice that lets whomever you're speaking to know, in no uncertain terms, that you are anything but compliant.

Washington glowered. He gnawed at the end of his thumb for a moment. He sighed. "It doesn't matter anyway. Even if these two are ready to be promoted to Santas," he gestured at Janika and Justus, "that's still only four Santas."

Randolph looked at Washington, face impassive.

Washington looked incredulous. "Oh, lord, man, no" he said. "No! No. No. No. No."

Randolph spread his hands. "We need five."

"We'll be lucky to have five minutes with that crazy old bastard around! He'll wreck everything."

"Sir," said Janika. "Everything is already wrecked."

Washington looked at her. He sighed. His eyebrows went up, then back down. He shook his head. "Well, at least you guys got me out of jail. Even if it was a pretty terrible jail break, especially for a group of wizards."

"That's the spirit," said Randolph. "Now. As soon as your clothes arrive, Bertram, we'll be off."

"Where are we going?" Daniel asked.

"We are going where one goes to find irascible and occasionally dangerous old wizards who may or may not have already tipped into dementia," said Randolph. "Florida."

CHAPTER 29

A suit arrived from the same store where Randolph had bought his. This one wasn't tweed herringbone though, it was pinstripe. Once Bertram had a shower and got dressed in it he looked like he might be the CEO of something, possibly the mayor of something. Maybe both.

"It does feel better to be dressed," he said. "You'll thank Gaffney for me, won't you Randolph?"

"He'd probably rather hear from you now that you're the top man," Randolph said.

"Who's Gaffney?" Daniel asked.

"He's the top men's clothier in Atlanta." Randolph said.

"I'll have to stop in when I get back," Daniel said.

Randolph and Washington looked at one another. Some meaning was exchanged, but Daniel couldn't decipher it.

"What?" he said.

Randolph ignored him, spoke to Bertram instead, who was adjusting a bit of silk in his breast pocket. "Excellent choice of square, by the way," he said.

"It's all about the color, I find," Bertram said.

"Too right." Randolph looked up, realized Janika, Daniel, Justus were all staring at the two of them.

"Should we go save the world now?" Janika asked.

"Now that we're dressed, yes," Bertram said.

Since the truck was gone, hopefully forever, they had the hotel's concierge arrange for a shuttle to the airport.

"We're going to have to fly commercial, I'm afraid," Randolph said.

"We do what we must," observed Bertram.

"How are we going to pay for a ticket to Florida?" Daniel asked. "Just walking into the airport and buying a ticket has to be like a million dollars. I mean, do I have to pay for myself? Because I never got paid at the mall and-"

"Not to worry," said Randolph. "I have a man."

After about 45 minutes of driving south through the city the taxi van navigated the ramps and exits that funneled traffic around the Atlanta airport. They arrived at the North Terminal, and Randolph stepped out of the van, then craned his neck back and forth until he spotted a squat man in a black suit hurrying their way.

Bertram paid the taxi driver. Everyone else got out as the man in the black suit was approaching with a big smile on his face and a clipboard under one arm.

"Ah, Scott, so nice to see you again," said Randolph.

Scott was very cheerful. He shook Randolph's hand. "You as well, Mr. Twisleham, you as well. These are the members of a new performing group, I'd imagine?" He cast his bright smile over Daniel, Janika, Justus.

"Indeed they are," said Randolph. "Just on our way down to Florida for some meetings with the label executives, you know."

"Oh yes, yes, of course," Scott said. "Well, let's be going then, shall we? Any luggage today?"

"No," Randolph replied. "Quick trip, down and back. This is Mr. Washington, by the way."

Scott shook hands with and shared his enthusiastic smile with Bertram, who nodded.

Scott held an arm out to indicate they should all enter the airport, then turned and walked briskly through the automatic doors.

Daniel began loosening his belt, then removed it from the loops.

"What are you doing?" Janika asked.

"It's the airport. You have to take your belt and shoes off or they won't let you on the plane," he said.

"That won't be necessary this time," Scott said, with a laugh. "Sorry, I should have said something already."

Janika gave Daniel a weird look as if to say, "See, you fool?"

Daniel looked back at her as if to say, "Trust me, this sort of thing happens. I was right to be taking my belt off."

Justus stared straight ahead as if to say, "I am a bottomless black abyss who cares nothing about anything."

They walked through the ticketing area, into a wide roundish room with shops and restaurants around the perimeter. Daniel was familiar with this room, having flown out of Atlanta before. It was known as the "atrium" and it was usually where a very long wait to get through security began. Indeed, there were two long lines here that reached into the distance to the group's right and ended in a barely-visible maze of temporary posts with ropes attached between them to control the flow of passengers.

Scott walked briskly around the tail end of the lines, then made a right and marched along the wall.

Daniel began to get nervous, and ran through his Impending Airport Security checklist in his mind. Was he carrying any liquids over four ounces? Or was it three ounces?

He couldn't remember but it didn't matter because he wasn't carrying any liquids. Was he carrying anything that the TSA might arbitrarily consider to be a weapon? Fingernail clippers? Keys? Bobby pin? Toothpick?

He patted at his pockets, felt like he might be OK. Then he realized with cold dread that he was definitely still missing something.

"Uh, Randolph," he said.

Randolph looked over his shoulder at Daniel and shook his head as he walked.

Daniel knew that meant he should shut up, but they didn't have tickets. There was no way they were going to get on an airplane without boarding passes. He couldn't help himself. He hissed into Randolph's ear, "Tickets. We don't have tickets."

Randolph gave him a pointed, eyebrows-up look that clearly said "would you please shut up and be patient? I have this all well in hand."

Daniel shrugged.

As they got closer to the front of the security line, Daniel thought certainly that Scott was going to pull aside one of the ropes and let them into the front of the line, which was a nice time saver but didn't do anything to alleviate the fact that none of them had tickets. Instead, Scott merely waved to the nearest TSA employee, then took a left down a corridor, and then pushed open a door to his right, letting bright sunlight stream in. They descended a set of metal stairs that crisscrossed back on themselves until they led down to the tarmac itself where a black van with blacked out windows waited.

Scott jumped into the van. Randolph took the front seat. Everyone else piled in behind. The van's seats were a nice leather, each one its own discrete seat; no bench seats.

Once everyone was in, Scott began to drive along the

tarmac, weaving in between planes, piles of equipment, and trains of cars stacked with luggage.

"So what are they called?" he asked.

"I'm sorry?" Randolph said.

"This new group, what are they called? My kids are probably big fans of theirs,"

"Oh! Of course. We're not firm on a name yet. Just the planning stages, you know," said Randolph. "When we come through next time if we've had any success we'll have some T-shirts and so forth, if you like."

"That would be great," Scott said. "One of the perks of the job is being able to bring stuff to my kid."

Daniel thought that was unlikely. There was something about the way this Scott guy was talking that made Daniel think he might shepherd famous people through the airport all the time, and that he might have a side business going where he auctioned off whatever signed memorabilia he got his hands on using Internet bidding sites.

"It would be my pleasure," said Randolph.

The van stopped next to another set of stairs that went back up to the airport terminal level. Daniel hadn't known it before — though it made a lot of sense now that he thought about it — but the airport terminal was several stories in the air with all manner of support personnel and equipment below.

They all ascended the stairs. Scott swiped a card at a card reader and the door opened on the airport concourse. After a short walk, they'd arrived at a gate with several uniformed employees typing away at computer terminals.

"If you'd like to have a seat, this will just be a moment," Scott said.

They stood and watched Scott walk around the line of people waiting at the desk to talk to the airline representatives. He whispered in a lady's ear, which visibly annoyed the passenger on the other side of the desk from her. The airline lady held up a finger to the passenger to ask him to hold on for a minute, which only made him more annoyed. She nodded, typed furiously at the terminal, then smiled and nodded at Scott, who thanked her and smiled back. He collected some paper at a printer behind the counter, then motioned at the group to come with him.

He ran each of the pieces of paper, in turn, through a machine near the door to the corridor that ran down to the plane. Everyone followed him down the ramp. Daniel felt exposed, like at any moment a TSA agent was going to come out of nowhere and tackle him for not following normal airline wait-and-intimidate procedure.

No one tackled him. In fact, they were the first people on the plane. Scott made sure they were all happy in their seats. Randolph and Bertram were side by side in first class, Justus got two seats on an exit row, and Daniel and Janika were behind him in two normal airplane seats.

After Scott had gone, Daniel turned to Janika and said loud enough for Justus to hear, "What the hell was all that?"

"What?" she asked.

"We just swept through the airport like we are famous or something,"

Janika shrugged.

"As far as he knows, we are," said Justus.

Daniel unbuckled his belt and got up. The plane was still empty of other passengers, so he walked easily forward to where Randolph and Bertram were sitting. Both had what looked like a cocktail sitting on trays in front of their seats.

"What was all that?" Daniel asked.

"Diplomacy, my boy," said Randolph. "You'll learn a measure of it someday yourself, I expect."

"Not quite enough diplomacy to get us all into first class, though huh?" Daniel asked.

"Daniel," Randolph said. "Don't be cross. We have to sit in first class."

"And why's that. Because it fits our story or whatever?"

"Oh no," said Randolph, raising his glass and clinking it against Bertram's glass, "It's because we're gentlemen."

Washington snorted, clinked back.

Daniel returned to his seat.

CHAPTER 30

When they landed in Ft. Lauderdale, Randolph arranged a shuttle to take them a few miles up the Florida Coastline to something called the Whispering Pines. Daniel was expecting a forest, or at least one tree, but Whispering Pines turned out to be a condominium building situated on a finger of habitable area that sat apart from the mainland. The condo building looked out over the Atlantic.

The shuttle dropped them at the front door and a man in a white suit welcomed them to Whispering Pines and asked which guest they'd like to see.

"We've come to visit Mr. Lemaitre, please," said Randolph.

All the color drained out of the man in the white suit's face. "I see," he said, lips twitching. "And will you, uh? That is, will you need me to accompany you up to Mr. Lemaitre's residence, or might you be able to find the way?"

As the man in the white suit was talking, a round man in a similar white suit was walking out the front door of the building. He overheard what the first man had said.

"Ah, Brian?" the round man said.

Brian's face looked like it wanted to crawl off his head and go live on the head of someone who didn't get into unfortunate situations such as the one in which Brian and his face found themselves at this moment.

"Yes, Mr. Farley?"

"Of course our guests would like you to accompany them." Mr Farley's smile looked like it had gone to business school at a community college.

"It's quite all right," said Randolph. "I am an old friend of Mr. Lemaitre. I can assure you he wouldn't be interested in enlarging problems."

Brian's eyebrows rose again. Daniel thought if he wasn't careful he was going to have a headache later from all these facial expressions. Clearly, Brian wanted to seize this excuse to not accompany the group upstairs. Bur Mr. Farley was looking pointedly at him. Brian waved at the group to follow him into the building. They did, then joined him in an elevator.

"Don't worry," said Randolph to Brian, "You can just point us in the correct direction from the elevator. There are only two doors on Mr. Lemaitre's floor, correct?"

"Yes that's right," said Brian, looking relieved. "But I'm pleased to say that it's my great pleasure to escort you to the correct door so that there can be no mistake." He then made some gesture then, which no one could see but Randolph.

Randolph turned his head up to look at the corner where the wall of the elevator met the ceiling. There was a camera there. Brian clearly thought that Mr. Farley was the kind of man to order a subordinate to do something, then go and watch the closed circuit camera footage to ensure the employee did as told.

Randolph smiled warmly at Brian. "The things we do for duty," he said. "Do you have any children, Brian?"

"I do, actually," said Brian. "Twin girls."

"They have a very smart father," Randolph observed.

"Thank you, sir," said Brain, in a tone that indicated that he hoped Randolph was right about that, for his sake as well as the girls'.

The elevator dinged then, and the doors parted to reveal a short, carpeted hallway. In the middle of the hallway sat a live, gigantic, male Bengal tiger. It made a low noise in its throat, and Brian said, "Ah, Jesus," under his breath. The tiger stood, growling now. It had to weigh a ton, all ripping muscle and teeth and claws. It was walking toward the elevator and glaring menacingly.

Randolph waved a hand and proclaimed, quietly, "Bollocks."

The tiger froze as if it was a movie and someone had pressed pause.

Bertram Washington grunted, then said, "You see what I mean about this guy? He really puts the 'dick' in 'unpredictable.'"

"Come along, Brian, you're in no danger, I assure you," Randolph said. He strode forward and walked directly through the form of the tiger as if it were an image projected on mist.

Brian whimpered as Randolph walked through the image of the animal, probably not sure of what he should be more afraid: that there was a tiger, or that it was a hologram of some kind. He followed, giving the tiger a wide berth.

As Brian passed the image, it turned its great head to look directly at him. Brian jumped straight up in the air and emitted a high-pitched shriek. Randolph was standing halfway down the hallway, having turned to see what the shriek was about. Brian, having reached top speed without requiring time or distance to do so, nearly knocked him down.

A door at the end of the hallway opened and a half dozen men dressed in black tactical clothing and carrying submachine guns boiled out, then began firing toward the elevator. Daniel, Janika and Justus all leaped to either side in the elevator for cover. The fire was deafening, then stopped abruptly.

Daniel peeked around the corner of the elevator. He expected to see carnage, blood, death.

Instead, he saw Brian, the condominium employee running at full speed into the elevator. Daniel dodged and Brian rebounded off the rear wall of the elevator and went down on his back, shrieking, "Guns! Guns! Tiger! Guns!" between panting breaths.

In the hallway, Bertram was turned away from the elevator. His shoulders were shaking and he appeared to be gripping his body with one arm. Bertram turned to look over his shoulder, saw Brian down in the elevator, then met Daniel's eyes and continued to laugh into his hand.

Randolph was looking at Bertram with disapproval. Behind him, the soldiers, or whatever they were, were paused like the tiger had been. Spent brass casings hung in midair. Several of the submachine guns were flashing as though they'd been stopped in mid shot.

Randolph wiped his hand at the hallway and muttered something to himself. The tiger and the army men disappeared.

Justus bent to check on Brian, then shrugged.

"Scared but fine," he said. He helped the man up.

Brian was gibbering wordlessly and staring into space. "T-," he said. "Tiger."

Randolph had returned to the elevator, drew out his globe, twiddled his fingers. Brian looked in a much better mood. Everyone exited the elevator, and Brian disappeared behind the closing doors, a smile on his face.

Randolph sighed.

Bertram was still laughing, no longer trying to conceal his amusement. "Hoo! Oh, mercy. I feel for that guy, but hearing him scream like that just slays me," he said. He leaned back and spread both his hands to mimic Brian's terror. "Aaah!"

Randolph arched an eyebrow at him.

Bertram's laugh stumbled a little. He looked sheepish, put his hands down. He wiped his eyes. "All right," he said, still smiling. "You're right. Conduct unbecoming a Santa Claus, you're probably right."

"What was all of that?" Daniel asked. He felt a little emotionally drained himself.

"Security system," said Janika. "No wonder that Brian guy never wanted to come up here."

Randolph nodded at her. "He wouldn't ever remember what he saw up here, but he'd definitely remember that he hated coming up to this hallway. I'm willing to bet his boss, Mr. Farley, has never been down this hallway, or he'd understand our friend Brian's misgivings."

"So now what?" Daniel asked.

"Well, now we're through the outer layer of security," Randolph said.

"Outer layer? There's more?" Daniel asked.

Randolph shrugged. "Probably. Let's ask."

He strode toward the end of the hall. Daniel braced for something else awful to happen. Bertram Washington, clearly enjoying himself, let out a small giggle.

Randolph raised his fist to knock on the door, but before he could, it jerked open and a small, elderly man leaped out.

"How'd ya like that tiger, Randy, you dirty old fuck?" the man shouted, his voice half a wheeze. On the word "fuck," a plume of fire shot out the back of his pants with a loud bang. There was a smell of rotting soup and burning cloth.

Daniel jumped.

"Whoo! That was a good one!" Lemaitre shouted, then laughed a raspy laugh.

"It's a pleasure, Erasmus," said Randolph. "Everyone, meet Erasmus Lemaitre, retired Santa." Erasmus Lemaitre was a stooped, white-haired gnome. He wore a green stocking cap on his head with ghostly wisps of hair protruding at all angles. His chin was white stubble. He wore a plaid flannel shirt and a pair of khaki trousers pulled up nearly to his nipples.

"Retired like hell," Erasmus shouted. Perhaps he wasn't shouting, Daniel thought. Maybe this was just his normal speaking voice. "I was shoved out by that son of a bitch right there!" said Lemaitre. He poked at the air in Bertram's direction with his cane.

"You were a danger to yourself and others," Bertram said. "You still are. God help us if you blast a hole in your pants near a gas station."

"You fish-lipped son of a whore!" Lemaitre rasped, getting even louder. "I'll stove your head in with my cane and use it as a whiskey cup!" He was jabbing his cane with each syllable now, and shuffling forward a half step at a time toward Bertram. "Your head, that is. Obviously I can't use my cane as a whiskey cup, you shit-livered cabbage!"

Ah, Daniel thought. This was definitely yelling.

Randolph put a hand out and stopped Erasmus's advance. Randolph didn't have a particularly big hand but it looked enormous on the old gnome's chest.

"Actually, Erasmus, we're here to ask you to join us," said Randolph. "There's something we need to do. A task with which only you can help."

"Is it ripping Washington's head off and kicking it so hard that it fucks off into space?" Erasmus screamed. His eyes were wide and slightly yellow. Flecks of spittle flew as he yelled.

"You'd break half the bones in your body if you tried, old man," observed Bertram. "And I'd break the other half."

There was a pause, then Erasmus backfired again. Daniel now realized why Randolph was standing slightly to the side. He'd known it was coming.

If Daniel were a betting man and Erasmus made it close enough to Bertram to initiate any sort of physical contest, he'd have put his money on Bertram for sure. Bertram wasn't a young man, but he was definitely muscly. Erasmus Lemaitre looked winded from the effort of holding up his clothes.

"No," said Randolph. "In fact, we're going after Krampus."

That brought Erasmus up short. He studied Randolph's face.

"Ya what now, sonny?" he asked.

Randolph nodded. "It's happening," he said.

"Well, why dintcha say so?" Erasmus asked. He lowered his cane and began shuffling back toward his front door. "Come on inside. There's lemonade," he said.

CHAPTER 31

The inside of Erasmus's condo was a mixture of different styles that didn't so much clash as wreck into each other. There was a chair and a sofa which were pea green corduroy. In a glass case, several obviously magical nicknacks swirled, flashed, and sparkled. On the wall was a gigantic television that was paused in the middle of a golf game.

"Ya like golf, sweetheart?" Erasmus spoke/yelled when he saw Janika looking at the big TV.

"I've never played," she said. She looked like she didn't quite know what to think and didn't much care for being called "sweetheart," but in the interest of progress was going along.

"Think it's boring as fuck, don't ya?" Erasmus shouted, then dissolved into a series of spasms that would have sent any EMT scrambling for their medical bag, but which Daniel now knew to be his absurd laugh. At the end of these, Erasmus lifted his ancient, bony posterior from his chair so that the explosion resulting from his use of the word "fuck" would miss his chair.

Even though he was ready for the bang this time, it still made Daniel wince when it came.

"Well, I'll tell ya honey," Erasmus went on. "It's a lot of fun if you know how to play. Watch this!" He waved a spindly hand at the television and it un-paused itself. Daniel filed this motion away for later. Could he learn to manipulate televisions without a remote through magic? What a time saver that would be. The money he wouldn't have to spend on batteries alone was worth looking into it.

Erasmus lifted a fist to his mouth and blew into it, then opened it with a flourish. A big white bird popped into existence with a small attendant puff of feathers. Erasmus grabbed for the bird, which squawked, flapped, was caught. The old wizard then threw the bird over his head in a basketball-style hook shot at the huge sliding glass doors which looked out over the ocean.

Daniel was expecting the bird to rebound painfully off the glass, but instead it shot straight through, leaving a quickly expanding ripple behind as though the glass were water. The bird then flapped, righted itself and flew away.

Erasmus turned to look at everyone as if to say, "How about that, huh?"

"Um," said Janika.

Erasmus lifted a finger, then leveled it at the TV. On screen, a man was lining himself up for a shot on the green, holding up his golf bat to judge whatever people who hold up golf bats use them to judge. As he squatted to eyeball his shot even further, a large white bird landed next to his ball, grabbed it in its beak, then shit on the green and flew away with the ball. The golfer watched the bird fly away with slack-jawed wonder.

Erasmus was again consumed with his disturbing version of laughter. Everyone else laughed too, even Bertram, who muttered, "Not bad, heh."

"Wait," said Daniel. "You had that paused for a few minutes, so, that wasn't even happening live. Did the bird go back in time, or–"

Erasmus glared at Daniel, then said, to Bertram, "He must be your apprentice."

"Not mine," said Bertram.

"Blaaaah," said Erasmus, with the wave of a bony hand.

Randolph swept in with a tray in his hand bearing a teapot and cups. "Here we are," he said. "My compliments to our host for having some proper tea."

Erasmus accepted a tea cup, then worked his mouth for a few seconds before trying a sip of it. Then he said, "Ooh that's quite nice," speaking quietly for the first time as far as Daniel knew.

"Let's get down to business," suggested Randolph, settling into a creaky wooden chair that looked like it had belonged to a dining room set at some stage of its life.

The plan was explained to Erasmus, who grunted and sipped his tea as he listened. When Randolph was done speaking, Erasmus said, "It might work, in that you'll probably get yourselves killed, but I don't know where you're gonna get five Santas if Krampus has already destroyed the order. Even if I agree to join you, which is VERY MUCH IN QUESTION..." Erasmus yelled these last four words pointedly at Bertram, paused, then continued. "Even then, that's only three."

"Justus and Janika are ready," Randolph said, gesturing at the two who sat side by side on a steamer trunk. This might have been the most guests Erasmus's condominium had ever seen, and was certainly more than it could accommodate with good seating.

Erasmus moaned at the sight of the two prospective Santas, as did Bertram. Then they look at each other, realized they agreed about something, looked away.

"Well then," said Erasmus. "I am prepared to join you in this likely fruitless, certainly ill-advised question," he paused theatrically. "If Bertram is willing to kiss my bony old ass. Literally kiss it. Lips to cheek."

"Like hell, you old fossil," Bertram said.

"Gentlemen, I remind you that the fate of our order, and by extension, the fate of our entire world hangs in the balance," said Randolph.

Erasmus sighed noisily and unhappily. "You are right," he said. "I suppose I will accept that he merely pats my bony old ass lovingly with one hand."

CHAPTER 32

In the end, it appeared that Erasmus merely wanted to make Bertram squirm a little, because when it was time to go the old man appeared quite pleased. He led everyone down the elevator to the lobby, then had Randolph hold the elevator doors while he went to let the concierge know he'd be gone a couple of days.

When Erasmus returned, he got back on the elevator and they descended once more level to a garage area where a van was parked. He withdrew keys from his pocket and tossed them to Randolph, who got into the driver's seat. Bertram took the passenger seat, Erasmus the first bench, and then Janika, Justus, and Daniel in the back few seats.

Randolph pulled out onto the highway, headed north.

"Wow," said Daniel. "It's lucky you have this van we can all fit in."

"What's that sonny?" Erasmus yelled, cupping a hand around his ear.

"I say, it's lucky you have a big van all of us can fit in," said Daniel, enunciating clearly on each syllable.

"Nonsense, we just stole this heap of junk," Erasmus said.

He laughed. "Hope you like it too, because if we're driving to HQ we're gonna be in here a couple of days."

"I rather think we can get there faster than that," said Randolph. "Daniel is a teleporter."

"Is he really?" Erasmus asked.

"He is," confirmed Randolph.

"Which one's Daniel?" Erasmus asked.

Daniel raised his hand.

Erasmus twisted in his seat and eyed Daniel, then thrust his face forward to look closely in Daniel's eyes. Daniel smelled soup again. Erasmus's yellowed, veiny eyes darted back and forth between Daniel's pupils.

"Yes, yes, I see that he is," said the old man. His breath was very nearly the worst thing Daniel had experienced since being attacked at the mall.

"Daniel, would you mind terribly if Erasmus were to-" Randolph began. But he was cut off by Erasmus, who yelled "No time like the present! Fuck it!"

Erasmus grabbed at Daniel and slapped his bony old hand atop his head. As soon as he did, Daniel was twisted from the feet up. It felt like his body was being stretched and stretched, infinitely long. At first he felt a sort of exhilaration in his chest, but the feeling rose quickly, without end. Soon it was sheer terror. Lights shot over him, through his body, burning him where they touched him, consuming his entire being.

He felt somehow that he was being crushed into the revolting old soup-and-stale-farts smell that was Erasmus, like they were sharing the same space, becoming one being. He could have sworn that he heard a sound like the cackling of an ancient man's laughter, but that could also have just been some facet of the crackling roar that was assaulting his ears. Supposing he still had ears, that was.

The roar crashed to a crescendo, mirroring the terror, and then, nothing.

It was as though Daniel were loosed from whatever horror had been gripping him. He drifted, soulless and without form. There was sunlight. Someone was holding him, whispering in his ear, lips brushing his earlobe. He felt warmth, comfort, happiness.

His eyes fluttered open. There was sunlight but no warmth. He must have blacked out. When he regained consciousness he was looking upward at the interior ceiling of the van with Justus looking down at him.

The big man looked very unhappy. Seeing that Daniel's eyes were open, he nodded, then backed out of the van.

Daniel sat up. He couldn't tell where they were. They'd been transported to another planet or something. Everything here was white. The sun was hot, he was sweaty, but when the wind blew it was horribly cold. Janika was nearby. She mouthed, "You OK?" at him. He nodded.

Justus marched over to Erasmus, towered over him.

"What do you want, you big gorilla?" Erasmus rasped.

"I understand that you are a man who used to be respected," said Justus. He waved a hand at Randolph and Bertram. "Perhaps you still are by these men. But if you lay hands on my friend again, use his magic without his permission, you will need every ounce of your magic to protect yourself from me."

Erasmus blustered. "What are you talking about? An apprentice questioning my methods? Twisleham, are you going to stand there and let your boy talk to me this way? I thought we were saving the Earth, not twaddling around with apprentices and their applicant friends. Humph."

Justus leaned down to look the old man in the eye. "You are not talking to them right now, Erasmus Lemaitre. I know your name, and you are talking to me."

Erasmus clearly didn't want to look Justus in the eye, but, reluctantly, he did.

"Well, I ah," the old man stammered. Something he'd seen in Justus's stare rattled him. "Yes I see that you, er. Are quite powerful and will make a fine Santa. Yes indeed. A fine Santa."

Justus nodded. "Let us carry on then," he proclaimed.

"Indeed," said Randolph.

"Aren't I supposed to be leading you bunch of crazies?" Bertram asked.

"Do you want to be in charge?" Randolph said.

"Hell no," said Bertram.

"Excuse me," said Daniel. "What just happened?"

"Erasmus used your power to teleport the entire van. We are above the arctic circle," Janika said.

"People can use other people's powers?" Daniel asked. "That's gotta be like, thousands of miles. You can teleport that far?"

"Apparently so," said Janika.

"Let's get out of the cold before we freeze to death," said Randolph.

"Why aren't we frozen already?" Daniel asked.

"We will be soon," Janika said.

"All right, give me a minute," said Erasmus. He closed his eyes, muttered irritably, waved his arms. Then he shuffled forward a few steps. There was a popping sound. Daniel couldn't tell exactly where it had come from, but there was something about the sound that gave him the impression that it was very loud, but far away.

"Shit!" yelled Erasmus. Daniel had never seen the old man standing facing away. His trousers were blasted out in the back and two pale white butt cheeks hung inside, swaying softly. They were briefly obscured by a small electrical storm that sounded like cheap firecrackers.

Erasmus waves his arms some more, shuffled a bit more. "There we go," he said.

"There we what go?" Bertram asked.

"Give it a minute," Erasmus said.

Quietly, to Janika, Daniel said, "What is his magic exactly?"

"I don't know," she whispered.

"He can manipulate all forms of electromagnetism," said Randolph.

Just then there came another popping sound. This time there was no question that the sound was loud. The ground, made up of ice and snow, began to buckle outward as though a giant mole were surfacing from underneath. Huge blocks of ice fell away as a column of what looked like dense black metal rose from the ground. There were metal ladder rungs in the side.

Daniel had seen enough war movies to guess what he was looking at.

"A submarine?" He stared. His mouth was open, so he closed it. "So, wait. Santa Claus really does live at the north pole, but it's in a submarine?" he asked.

Randolph shrugged. "Best way to never be found is to keep moving," he said.

"And for what it's worth, I live in Atlanta," Bertram said. "This is just my work's main office."

CHAPTER 33

Upon seeing the inside of the submarine, Daniel was having several problems. These problems all centered around his preconceived notions. First, there was his notion of what a Santa was like, and what Santa's workshop at the North Pole was like. None of that appeared to be congruent with reality, as had been proven abundantly clear over the last few days.

Next, there was his notion of what the inside of a submarine should look like, which was now at odds with his surroundings. He was standing in a half-moon shaped room that was dimly lit by lights from above, as well as some lights at ankle level sat in the wall. The roof of the area was arched, following the curve of the outer hull of the ship.

Justus descended the ladder, having made sure the door was shut. *It probably wasn't called a "door,"* Daniel thought. *Hatch? Did they call it a hatch? That sounded right.* Whatever it was called, Justus had shut it and was now standing with everyone else in the submarine's — for lack of a better word — foyer.

"Welcome all, to our most secret headquarters," Randolph said. "Everyone has been here except you, Daniel, I believe."

Daniel noticed that he did not use the words "Santa's Workshop."

The floor moved under Daniel's feet.

"We are diving now, in order to keep moving. Even though it's clear that our entire order has been compromised, it's important to maintain some sense of protocol, I think," Randolph said.

"Whatever you say, fancy pants," Erasmus said. "What's next?"

"We'll have a ceremony for Janika and Justus to welcome them to the full rank of Santa, and then a small celebration. Normally we'd have an evening of drinking and merriment but in this case we shall have to truncate for time."

"Yes, let's move it along, shall we?" Erasmus said.

Justus turned his great head to look at the old gnome.

"I, er," the old man said, sounding a bit like he was stammering. "I mean, in the interest of locating Krampus and removing him from whatever he's up to."

Randolph nodded. "As you say. Janika, Justus, if you want to show Daniel to the reading room, we'll prepare for you two." He smiled. He was apparently doing his best to maintain whatever circumstance and gravitas would normally befit someone rising to the rank of Santa even though they were rushed.

Janika nodded, walked toward a double door a few steps away. She motioned at Daniel, who followed. Justus brought up the rear. As she got close, the door slid open to reveal a hallway. It was a lot longer than Daniel thought it should be, but he hadn't seen any of the submarine's body under the ice, just the part that had the front door.

She turned left down a second hallway and they stepped into a wood-paneled library with vaulted ceilings and stained glass windows that glowed in the rays of the afternoon sun.

This submarine must be enormous, Daniel thought.

"It's not that big," Janika said, elbowing him in the ribs. Then she splayed the fingers of both her hands and said, "Magic!"

Justus flopped down on one of the couches arranged in a U shape. Janika sat on another. Daniel walked to the rows of books and read some of the titles. *Transmutation the Easy Way. Transmogrification: Not Just for Kids with Tigers.* He backed up a little. There was a whole section on teleportation. He'd have to read those. Maybe there were some books on how to prevent people from using your magic without your permission as well. That had been intensely uncomfortable.

Daniel turned. "I have to tell you guys, I really don't like that Erasmus dude," he said.

Janika made a face. "I don't either," she said. "I know we need him, and he seemed harmless enough, but he smells bad."

"That is true," said Justus. "Like a soup made with piss."

"You guys didn't have to mix magic with him. It was horrible." He was quiet a moment, thinking about how bad it was. "So, you guys have been here before? Is it normally like this?"

"Like what" Janika asked.

"Well, empty," Daniel said.

Janika looked around. "Yeah that's actually pretty frightening now that you mention it. We'll have to ask Randolph about it."

"Ask me about what?" Randolph said, rounding the corner. He smiled, then added, "It's so wonderful when timing works out nicely like that, isn't it?

"Have you noticed that this place seems awfully empty?" Daniel asked.

"I have," Randolph said. "From what I can tell, they've

been turned to work with the forces of Krampus, forgotten the order, or..." he trailed off. Daniel thought this might be because he couldn't think of a third option, or because he could and he didn't want to say it out loud.

"So this submarine was just running on auto pilot?" Daniel asked.

"Something like that," Randolph said. He smiled. "Now, if you'll all join me in the Great Hall, we have a ceremony to attend."

Justus and Janika stood. They smiled at each other. Janika hugged her brother, then they followed Randolph back down the hallway, through the entrance area — since it probably wasn't called the submarine's foyer — and then through an opposite set of double doors. These led down a set of stairs to a cavernous room that looked somewhat like a church, somewhat like a theatre. There were rows and rows of seats surrounding a stage which projected out into the audience and connected with the stairs on the far end.

Randolph paused at the top of the stairs, then descended them in a slow pace, presumably to add majesty.

Bertram and Erasmus waited on the stage below. Bertram was wearing what Daniel would have called a pope hat. It was round at the bottom but looked a little bit like a tulip toward the middle and the top. He was also holding a staff with a crooked end, like a shepherd, or like Jesus in one of those religious paintings. Erasmus was wearing the same clothes as before. He looked like he didn't want to be doing this at all. Maybe he didn't like ceremonies, or something.

Behind the two men was a table with a green cloth draped over it with mystical symbols embroidered into it. On the table was a black wooden chest that looked very old.

"Who brings these hopefuls before us?" Bertram asked in a grand voice.

"I do," proclaimed Randolph, similarly grand.

As Randolph, Janika and Justus were walking on to the stage proper, Randolph gestured that Daniel should sit in one of the front row seats. He did.

Bertram was glaring at Erasmus.

"Er," wheezed Erasmus. He got a piece of paper out of his pocket, unfolded it, looked at it, put a pair of glasses on.

Bertram was still glaring. He tapped on Erasmus's paper with his finger.

"Nguh," said Erasmus. He was acting like his throat hurt, or something. "I said I don't want to do this," he said, finally, irritably.

Bertram looked like he was going to explode. Veins stood out on his head and his eyeballs looked ready to pop out of his face and slam into Erasmus.

"Do we all agree that these acolytes are ready to assume the rank of Santa?" Randolph asked.

Bertram glared at Erasmus a second longer, who didn't look up from studying his paper. Finally, Bertram turned to Randolph. "We do," he said.

Bertram poked Erasmus in the arm with the round end of his staff.

"We do," said the old gnome, sounding sullen.

Janika and Justus looked at one another. Daniel thought Janika might be crying. She held her brother's hand.

"In said agreement, then, let it be so," said Bertram. He brought his staff down on the hard surface of the stage and it made a loud, ringing noise quite a bit louder than Daniel would have guessed it would make.

Janika jumped and hugged Justus this time. She turned and flashed a smile at Daniel, who waved back.

Randolph was smiling. "Right, well, I'm sorry that the circumstances are so peculiar, but you two definitely deserve the rank," he said.

"Let's get on with the rings already," wheezed Erasmus, now back to his normal too-loud volume.

Bertram was glaring again. "Don't you think they should have a little time to relax?"

"They did, while we were preparing for this," said Erasmus. "Now we are wasting time. We are all that's left of our order!"

Bertram grumbled.

"It's OK," said Janika. "We can celebrate after we deal with Krampus."

"Yes," said Justus. "I agree."

Randolph shrugged. "Very well, then." He gestured toward the black box on the table. Erasmus reached for it, tried to open the lid. It wouldn't budge.

"That's peculiar," said Randolph. "Should open for any Santa. You've been officially reinstated..."

"Blasted thing," muttered Erasmus.

Bertram reached for the box, pushed on the top of the lid, and it opened easily. Inside was red cloth that had probably once been brightly colored, but, due to age, had dulled somewhat. Five slots held five rings of a dull yellow metal. Each person removed one, held it, turned it over in their hands.

"So how does this work?" Janika asked.

"I have no idea," said Bertram. "I wasn't around when this magic was created."

"We just touch the rings together," said Erasmus. "Come on, let's get on with it."

"That's it? We just touch them together and then we find out where Krampus is?" Janika asked.

"We don't have to," said Erasmus. "I could just call out for him."

"There's not need to be sarcastic," Janika said.

Daniel thought it would have been much more majestic if they'd all been able to hold their rings overhead and touch them together that way, but because Erasmus was so diminutive, not to mention stooped in his old age, they had to touch them together where he could reach.

"Tally ho," said Randolph. His ring was the last to meet the others. When it did, there was a tiny metallic "Ting!" but nothing else.

Then, from out of nowhere, laughter. Deep, foreboding laughter.

CHAPTER 34

There was a boom. Daniel tried to crane his neck to see if he could see what was happening, but found that he couldn't move any of his body. He could breathe, he could use his eyeballs, but he couldn't move his limbs.

On the stage, everyone else seemed similarly afflicted. They were all frozen in their places. Behind the group on stage, light was playing off something moving in the shadows. Whatever it was seemed to be the source of the laughter.

As it stepped out on the stage, Daniel realized that whatever he was looking at must be Krampus. The beast was enormous, covered in red hair, and with large, fiery eyes set into a massive head that looked like it belonged to a goat, except that no goat could be that big. Thick horns curved backward from its brow. A thick chain was looped over its shoulders that jingled as it walked on to the stage, laughing.

It had hands like a human. One of them was outstretched as it walked. The other held what looked like a piece of a bush or tree branch. Its lower half was that of a goat as well, except for the red fur. Instead of feet, the beast had black hooves with a mirror shine, just like the curving black horns atop its head.

It was still laughing. On stage everyone was struggling against their frozen bodies.

"Bertram! Can you cast-" Randolph said.

"Nothing! I can't manage to ... argh" said Bertram. He must be trying to use magic, but was blocked somehow.

"What I love about you morons is," Krampus said, its voice deep and dark as his hooves thunked down on the stage. "You are so, utterly predictable. It's almost a chore to trap you like this. It's so obvious that it will work." He was close now, towering over the wizards, shaking his great head.

Erasmus somehow overcame the magic freezing the others on stage and Daniel's heart leaped in his motionless chest. Surely the old wizard could use some magic against this thing to break the others free. But he didn't use any magic. He just tossed his metal ring back into the ceremonial box it had come from, then plucked the other rings from the other hands and put them back as well.

"Erasmus what are you-" began Bertram. "You-" he started again. Then, finally, just said, "You!" Despite being frozen in place, Bertram's eyes were fixed on Erasmus as though he could bore a hole through the man with force of his gaze alone.

"I told you, didn't I, Washington?" said the gnarled old man. "I told you, you hadn't heard the last of old Erasmus. It's only sweeter now that it worked out this way. You, the last Santa Claus there will ever be." He chuckled.

"I thank you for your assistance, Lemaitre," boomed Krampus. "I was well on my way to wiping these trivial morons out, but this has worked out quite nicely with your help."

"I thought making them touch the rings together was a

bit heavy-handed, myself," said Erasmus. "Should have let me just kick Randolph in the plums or something."

"You have no sense of theatre," Krampus said.

"You despicable old wretch. I vouched for you." said Randolph.

"Oh, save it for someone who's listening, Twisleham," the old man spat. "Haven't you noticed already? You lost. The Santas are no more. People don't care about cooperation, about reason, about empathy. They care about their hand-held telephones, and their face-o-grams or whatever it's called. You were going down the drain anyway. My big red friend here offered me a considerable amount of money and a place in his organization, and all I had to do was help sell out the bastards who kicked me to the curb."

"You know very well why you were removed, Erasmus. Dress it up however you like. We swore to keep it secret, but you know," said Randolph.

Erasmus humphed.

"It was stealing, I believe," said Krampus. "He used his magic to manipulate bank records, teller machines, even some voting machines in local elections in some cases. Quite disgusting."

Erasmus's face was the picture of shock. "What? I never. Why would you say those things? I might have changed a red light or two in my favor when driving, but where's the harm in that?"

"Did you really think, Erasmus, that I would welcome a slimy, deceitful, twisted old snake like you into my organiza-tion?" Krampus asked. He leaned his horned head down to tower over Erasmus.

"Your organization is built upon lies and deceit!" Erasmus cried, cowering.

Krampus stood. "True," he said. "But I don't like you." The beast extended a red finger, grunted something unintelligible, and a wrist-thick bolt of energy shot toward Erasmus. There was a painful clap of noise, then Erasmus clutched his chest where a scorch mark blackened it. The old man staggered, then fell into a heap. His cane clattered to the ground.

"Hah!" laughed Krampus. "What a prick, am I right?" He reached into Randolph's pocket and withdrew the snow globe, saying, "I'll take that." Then he snatched the shepherd's crook from Bertram. "And that." He also plucked Janika and Justus's items off them, then threw them to the stage floor in a heap. He grunted with the effort of lifting his powerful leg into the air, then brought his hoof down and crushed everything there to bits. Water from inside Randolph's snow globe ran in tiny rivulets.

When Krampus lifted his hoof again, everything underneath was indeed smashed. He gave a satisfied grunt.

"I suppose you're going to kill us, now that you've disarmed us," Bertram said. "Cowardly, even for you."

Krampus turned slowly to regard Bertram and the remainder of the frozen wizards. He twiddled fingers at them and muttered, then said, "Perhaps I will, yes. If I have to. But I did not beat you by wasting resources. First I will, of course, determine if you can be used once I have controlled your minds."

As he was speaking everyone on stage put their arms down at their sides and stepped into line, then began walking toward the back of the auditorium, where they'd entered with Randolph.

"You'll never be able to manage it," Randolph said. His voice sounded strained, like he was attempting to break his bonds somehow, even though Daniel had no idea what to strain against, let alone how he might succeed.

As the group walked past Daniel's seat, he also stood up, though he had not commanded his body to do anything of the sort. It was an intensely off-putting sensation. It wasn't painful, as such, but it was jarring, as if his will was being bruised by his body moving without him asking it to.

"Don't be absurd, Twisleham. I've already managed it. Don't you see it in motion?" The beast noticed Daniel then, bent down, and plucked the watch from his arm, snapping the wrist band, and threw it onto the stage. The wrist band broke off completely and skittered away. Daniel could smell Krampus now. He smelled like camp fire, dirt, ash.

"Wouldn't want you doing any serious magic, would we, little adept?" The beast asked.

Daniel, moving like a robot, got into line behind Justus. They marched out of the hall and back down into the hallway.

"I'm most proud of the way I have embraced and enlarged the Christmas season," mused Krampus, as they walked. "Every year it gets longer and longer. More and more capitalism. More things bought on credit. More electronic gadgets, more games, more empty heads. It pleases me so. All that's left is to sink this stupid submarine with you in it."

"So we're to be crushed to death on the bottom of the ocean?"

"Possibly," said Krampus. "That would be nice. But I think it more likely that you will starve. I'm not sure it's deep enough here to actually crush this stupid thing. Whatever magic was put on it long ago is strong enough that I haven't been able to destroy it myself, but it will make a fitting tomb."

They were turning now, down a side corridor, into a section that was decorated — if the word "decorated" could be used at all — more in line with what Daniel would have expected from a submarine. There were no automatic doors here, just metal walls with thick metal doors that were round at the top and bottom. His legs lifted his feet and ducked his head to get through the port.

On the wall was painted the word "Brig."

There were three small rooms with heavy doors set into the curve of one wall. Bertram, Randolph, and Janika each walked into one of them. The doors slammed behind them. Daniel never saw a key. There might not even be one. There was also a cage with bars like a jail cell. Daniel walked into this and the door shut behind him.

"I have something special for you, big boy," said Krampus. Justus started walking again, then turned a corner. There was another metallic echo from somewhere else in the ship. Krampus came back, his heavy hooves pounding on the deck of the ship as he made his way back up the hallway, he opened a slot in Randolph's cell door and said, "Well that does it for me here, and you entirely, old boy. I have enjoyed besting you." Then he threw his great head back and laughed, slammed the slot closed, and pounded away down the hall.

Seconds later, the lights turned off, and Daniel was plunged into darkness. He turned his head to look for any source of light, but couldn't see anything. Then he realized that at least he had turned his head. That was an improvement over having his entire body controlled by a gigantic hellish red goat.

He found he was exhausted. He tried moving the rest of his body. Slowly it began to come back under his control. There was a faint sensation of pins and needles, like he'd slept on an arm wrong and deprived it of proper circulation, except that this time the feeling was over his whole body.

When he could move his whole body again, he felt around the cell. Against the back wall a metal ledge hung by some thick chains. He sat on it. He was exhausted, afraid, and functionally alone. He wanted to call out to see if any of the others could hear him but didn't want to summon Krampus back. What if the thing wasn't really gone? It might come back and do something terrible to him.

There was a terrifyingly loud bang then, which echoed down the hallway where Justus had been forced to march. The sound nearly made Daniel jump out of his skin.

Next he heard some small tapping sounds. He didn't know what those were either, but they sounded irregular. Maybe some machine was working nearby? Doing submarine stuff maybe?

There was a lurching sensation, and Daniel's world rotated a few degrees to his right. Oh no. They were headed toward the bottom of the sea. He had to do something. It was up to him to save his friends, then get back at this Krampus jackass for everything he'd pulled. He'd lost his watch, but he had an ace up his sleeve, so to speak. Krampus obviously didn't know that he could teleport.

There was another terrific bang. What could that be? Was Justus making that noise? Was someone shooting a gun? Maybe the submarine was knocking into the sea floor already, and there would be a rush of cold seawater to smother him.

Krampus had taken his watch, but he'd practiced teleportation without an instrument to help him focus. He could do this. He eyeballed the bars, trying to figure out how far he actually needed to go.

He felt exhausted, nowhere near the top of his ability. What if he used the magic, but ended up teleporting himself into the bars so they stabbed through his body? Surely that would be bad. Could that happen? He didn't know. He decided he'd better take some practice runs.

His eyes had adjusted to the dark now. He examined the bars. They were an inch thick, maybe two inches. When he'd practiced teleporting before, he'd been proud of how far he had gone, but if he really thought about it he might not have been able to transport himself far enough that he moved an entire body's distance, let alone his body's distance plus two inches.

If only someone could help him think through this, figure it out. BANG. The slamming noise came again. Daniel thought this time he'd also heard someone yell but couldn't be sure. The floor was pitched crazily now. He had to be careful.

He stood next to the bars, pressed his body against them so he'd have as little distance to travel as possible. His head hurt, but he ignored that thought, pushed it from his mind.

He concentrated, focused, pressed his body as hard into the bars as he could, and whispered, "Fuck." The rolling sensation came, like his whole body was a flag flapping in a sharp breeze. Then he opened his eyes and he'd done it! He was on the other side of the bars. He turned to look back into the cage he'd just been trapped in, but something around his waist was pulling at him.

Just then, there was a sickening rolling sensation, and the whole world shifted around him. He reached behind him, thinking his worst fears were realized and he'd managed to impale himself on the metal bars, but they'd just caught his jeans. He could probably pull free.

He pushed against the bars with all his might. There was a tearing sound, and he was free of the bars. There was another lurching movement of the floor, and he slammed his head against the metal wall of the nearby compartment. There was a fireworks display of sparks behind his eyes.

CHAPTER 35

When Daniel regained consciousness, Justus was again looming over him. The big man looked horrible. There was blood all over his face and neck, some of it still wet.

"Are you hearing me?" Justus asked.

"Yeah, yeah I hear you. Ow, my head hurts."

Justus nodded, stood. "Come on, we must free the others," he said.

"How did you get out?"

"I slammed myself into the door until it broke," Justus said.

That explained the banging sounds.

"Why are you bleeding?" Daniel asked.

"Because I slammed myself into a metal door until it broke," Justus said. "No problem."

They headed back into the auditorium to search for their magical items. Justus's pendant was broken, as was Daniel's watch. They both tried focusing on them, but to no avail.

Since that wasn't an option, they searched around until they found a closet with some tools in it, including a crowbar.

Justus used that to pry the metal doors open to release the rest of the crew.

Janika had been attempting to melt her door apart, as had Randolph. Janika had managed to get some melted area to show around the door's handle, and might have been ready to escape in another few days. Randolph had fared a little better.

"Oh," he said, when the door popped open. "I'd have had it open myself shortly."

Randolph and Bertram led everyone down the sloping walkways to a control room blanketed in blinking lights and readout screens.

"Oh great," said Bertram. "We're on the bottom of the ocean."

"Shouldn't be a problem. We have a teleporter," Randolph said, gesturing at Daniel.

"But none of us have our items anymore," said Daniel. "Krampus broke them all."

Randolph smiled. "Well, it's lucky that there are a few things Krampus doesn't know. First thing we need to do is get out of here, then we're going to show him just how much that is. Come with me."

Randolph led the way back into the auditorium. He gestured at the five metal rings stacked haphazardly on the wooden box where Erasmus had left them. He picked one up, held it up. It sparkled in the light, except there wasn't much light to sparkle in. It became clear that the ring was making its own sparkle.

"The beauty of these items is, not only will they still show us how to find wherever Krampus is hiding currently, they'll also work as magical totems for us. Pick one up and try it," he said.

Everyone else picked one up.

"Now focus your magic into it," Randolph urged. Sure

enough, they all sparkled at one spot in the ring just as Randolph's had. "If we follow that indicator, it will lead us to Krampus, and we can strike a blow at his very heart."

"But this will take forever," Bertram said. "We don't know how far away he is, only what direction we need to go to find his location."

Randolph didn't say anything, only pointed at Daniel.

"Ahh," said Bertram. "The teleporter."

"Precisely."

"I think we should get out of here," said Janika. "Didn't this sub crash into the ocean floor?"

"Oh," said Randolph. "Yes, you're right. It did. But I think we are somewhat safe, this being a very, very magical submarine. We're certainly in danger of being discovered out of our holding cells. Daniel, would you mind terribly helping us get out of here?"

"I don't mind but I'm pretty exhausted. I'm not sure if I could make it to the other side of the room at this point."

"Don't worry, you'll have quite a lot of power to draw on," said Randolph. "Rather more than you've used before, though, so we shall need to be careful. As long as we are all holding one of the rings, we can share magic."

"So we're like a giant robot made up of smaller robots?" Daniel asked.

Everyone blinked at him.

"If you like," said Randolph. Then they were gone.

CHAPTER 36

They popped into existence in what looked like an alleyway, except that it looked weird to Daniel. He couldn't figure out why it looked weird until he realized there wasn't any trash.

Thankfully, this time traveling as a group with someone else wielding his power to teleport wasn't nearly so terrible as when Erasmus had — for lack of a better word — stolen it from him. This time it was the same as when he used it himself, except it didn't tire him out at all.

"Where are we?" he asked.

"Frankfurt," Randolph said. He withdrew his phone from his pocket, thumbed at it a few times while looking at the ring he held in the other hand. Daniel could see he was trying to use his compass app.

"Takes a minute for it to start working when you skip thousands of miles like that," Randolph said.

"Mine takes that long to work in my own damn house," said Bertram.

"Here we are," said Randolph. "We are looking for something that is nearly directly southeast of us."

A man on a bicycle was riding down the alleyway, which, thanks to standing in a huddle, the five of them were blocking. The man stopped, got off his bike and looked expectantly at them.

"Was ist das?" he asked.

"Alles klar," Janika said.

They popped out of existence again.

This time they appeared in a park. Randolph was fiddling with his phone again.

"Where are we now?" Daniel asked. "Oh! And can we teleport into a bank and collect a bunch of money?"

"Doesn't really work out that well," said Bertram. "Even if you go in the vault, everything is in little locked boxes. And if you pop into the cashier's area they freak out and hit you with a shoe."

"This sounds oddly specific," observed Janika.

"We're in Brno, Czechia. Park Luzanky to be specific," Randolph said, without looking up. "Now our target appears southwest. I think I know where we're going already but let's be sure."

They disappeared again.

Now they were standing on a dirt road in the countryside somewhere. The air smelled like the sea.

"Is this Florida again?" Daniel asked.

"Heavens no," said Randolph. "With luck we'll never have occasion to return to that state. This is Italy. The Florida of Europe." He was fiddling with his phone still, then consulting his ring, holding it up, looking back at his phone.

"Bah," said Justus. "Russia is Florida of Europe. Everyone drinks too much, does stupid things. Italians just drive around comparing sun tans."

"He has a point," Bertram said.

"Do you mind if we focus on finding the target of our

investigation, and then continue with our effort to destroy the greatest threat to mankind, please?" Randolph asked.

"You mean can we be quiet while you diddle around with your cell phone?" Bertram asked.

"Yes," said Randolph.

"Aight," said Bertram. He shrugged at everyone else.

A breeze blew. It was salty and sweet. Daniel thought a stop by an Italian cafe for a cup of espresso would be very nice right now.

After a few more moments, Randolph looked up. "Alps," he said. "We're headed to the alps."

"When?" Daniel asked.

They disappeared again, and then were standing in a horseshoe-shaped parking lot by a large roundabout. Across the street was a big building with a green roof, as if it were made of copper and had corroded. Did people make roofs out of copper? Daniel didn't know.

Nearby their parking lot were some buildings that looked like offices or small businesses.

"Wait here," said Randolph. He strode toward the buildings.

The signs Daniel could see were in a language he couldn't understand.

"This is Germany," said Janika. "I can feel it." She frowned, then said, "Also, I can read the signs." She pointed to the retreating form of Randolph, who was opening the door to a small shop. "That one says 'Eagle's Nest Tours'" she said.

Daniel turned to look. Sure enough, it said "Eagle's Nest Tours," in English. He gave Janika a look. She winked at him.

"Wait, surely you don't mean 'Eagle's Nest' as in Hitler's private residence?" Bertram asked.

She shrugged. "I know as much as you do," she said.

Randolph was returning, unfolding a glossy piece of paper. He grunted at it, then folded it back up briskly. He looked at his ring again, consulted his cell phone. He told everyone they were about to move again. They did. He looked at the map, looked at his cell phone. "We're close," he said.

"Everyone down!" said Bertram, in a hoarse whisper. He pointed. A geist floated inches above the ground, bandages flapping in the light breeze. This one had a lot more bandages than the one they'd faced by the river in Alabama. Maybe it was a newer one? It also had two curs with it, both looking this way and that. One of them turned and looked directly at where Daniel was standing. His blood became frozen rain from a November rooftop.

Daniel hit the ground as everyone else was doing the same. They were in a grassy field with massive trees around some stone buildings. The geist seemed to have detected their presence, or perhaps heard the sound of them hitting the deck. Daniel could see that it was drawing closer. One of the curs howled. It might have been a howl, but it might also have been the shriek of someone being painfully tortured.

"Daniel, hold your ring," Randolph hissed.

Daniel looked down, when he'd dropped to the ground he'd let go of the gold ring. He grabbed at it. As soon as he had his hand on it, they disappeared again.

They reappeared in a very similar field, only this one didn't have a geist bearing down on them.

"Everyone up," said Randolph. They all got up. He was consulting his phone, then looking at his ring, then unfolding and peering at his map.

"This is the place," he said.

"What place?" Janika asked.

"Berghof," Randolph replied. "There must be some tunnels or catacombs or something similar around here."

Daniel heard shrieks in the distance. They sounded a lot like the ones the cur had been making a few minutes ago.

"So we're going to just walk in the front door?" Daniel asked.

Randolph tilted his head side to side. "Sort of, but I have an idea about that. We're going to get a little help."

CHAPTER 37

When they arrived in the yard of the Birchfield house it was beginning to get dark. Daniel knocked on the front door. Chris opened it, looking a lot healthier than he had previously, but also holding a beer and crunching a mouthful of chips.

Muromets peeked his massive head around the side of the house to see what the noise was. He too was crunching on something. Probably not chips.

"Ey!" Chris said. "If it ain't the magical Scooby Doo gang. Come on in."

They explained the situation.

"So basically," Chris said. "You're gonna attack Hitler's private residence from World War II and you want to rest up here and then take my giant away to do it?"

"Muromets does not belong to you," said Justus. "He belongs to himself."

"Take it easy, Giant Jr.," said Chris. "I'm just talkin' shit. But I do want y'all to take me with you."

"You understand that this will be a magical battle," said Randolph. "You aren't a magic user, by any chance?"

"Naw," said Chris. "I'm not. But I am two other things." He extended fingers to signify the two things. "One, I'm armed to the got-damn teeth. And two, I'm mad as hell at them fuckers for getting me hooked on meth, not to mention causing my aunt to shit her pants thinkin' I was-" he paused, then shook his head. "Well I was gonna say she was thinking I was hooked on drugs or something but she'd-a been right about that. Anyhow, if y'all're heading off to kick these shitheads in the dick I wanna do some kicking too."

"When you say armed to the teeth," Justus said. "How armed are we talking?"

Chris stood up. "I'll be right back," he said. He rushed off into the bedroom and could be heard rummaging around.

"I don't think this is a good idea," said Bertram.

"Because he's likely to get hurt?" Randolph asked.

"No, because he's clearly an unhinged redneck wacko," said Bertram.

"Ey," said Chris, in the doorway, holding two different rifles, both of which were painted matte black and looked extremely lethal. "I might be a redneck, but I am not unhinged. I been going to rehab and narcotics anonymous, I'll have you know."

Bertram held up both his hands. "OK, Sane Sammy. Show us your pea shooters then."

Chris smiled. He wiggled one of the rifles. "Well, this'n here isn't anything too special. It's your basic AR-15 variant with some very fancy electronic goodies attached to it, plus a collapsible stock and a short barrel. Real nice." He leaned that one in the corner next to the door. "But this," he said, holding the other, longer rifle in both his hands. "This here's a .50 caliber sniper rifle. You could shoot the nose of all four presidents on Mt. Rushmore if you lined this baby up right. 'Course, it'll cost you five bucks per shot cause the rounds are so fuckin' huge." He rattled the gun in both hands and made a laughing noise.

"How can you afford these guns? Aren't they expensive?" Daniel asked.

"Hell yeah they are. I went down across the river and poked around in the wreckage of the river house. It's pretty damn weird that's an airplane crash site and no one's come to look into it or anything, by the way. It's like as soon as those assholes who were running the drugs out of the house left, they forgot all about it."

"That's exactly what happened," said Randolph.

"Oh," said Chris. "Well that explains it then. And they ain't gonna be missing these guns."

"Be that as it may, I think we're going to have to pass," said Bertram.

"I'm not so sure," said Randolph. "Think about it, Bertram. What are our strengths? You and I are experienced wizards, but the rest of us are not. What we have on our side that they aren't likely to be prepared for is a giant, a fighter, a teleporter, and er, Chris." Randolph had possibly been going to say "redneck," but had thought better of it.

Bertram looked pained. He eyed Chris. Chris rattled his gun again. Bertram looked more pained. Finally, the Santa Claus sighed. "I guess we need everyone we can get," he said.

"Hell yeah!" said Chris. "So where we attackin' anyway?"

"You aren't gonna believe this." Daniel said.

"What?" Chris asked.

Randolph said, "We have reason to believe that Krampus's main base is in a tunnel system adjacent to the Berghof, the-"

Chris cut him off. His voice rose a few notches. If he'd seemed excited before, he was positively incandescent now. "The Berghof, like Hitler's summer house? You guys are fuckin' attacking Hitler's fuckin' summer house with fuckin' magic and I get to go along and shoot up some evil assholes?

Holy fuck I have never been so happy in all my got-damn life! Shit!"

"This is the kind of diatribe that makes me worry about you, son," said Bertram.

"Worry hell, I wish we could go back in time and kick Hitler himself right in the dick for America," Chris said.

Daniel had never seen him so happy or so animated.

"Let's all try to get some sleep, shall we?" asked Randolph. "We will spend tomorrow in preparation, then we go."

CHAPTER 38

"**R**ight," said Randolph, the next morning. He and Bertram were looking at Janika, Justus, and Daniel standing outside in the clearing where the meth lab trailer had been. Bertram's arms were crossed. He didn't look impressed.

"As long as we are linked by the rings," Randolph went on, "We each have access to the other's magic, and there's an additive effect as well, which means we can draw a lot more power together than any of us would be able to apart. Now, let's work on some fire, shall we?"

Janika went first. "Scheisse!" she yelled, reaching out with her hand. A gout of yellow flame arched forth into the morning air with a flickering shout of its own, then disappeared. Daniel could feel the heat on his face.

"Nicely done, Janika," said Randolph.

Bertram nodded.

Justus bent his knees, stuck his hand up. "Blyat!" he said. A thick column of fire shot out, almost like a laser. It looked like it could cut a bus in half. Maybe a line of buses.

"Very nice," said Bertram.

"Yes, for someone who isn't naturally a fire user, that was quite good," said Randolph.

"I like fire," said Justus.

Janika was eyeing him oddly.

"OK Daniel, let's see what you can do," Randolph said.

Daniel focused himself. He too bent his knees a little, since he'd seen Justus do it and it seemed like it might be a good idea. He put his hand up. "Shit!" he yelled.

A flame shot out, but there wasn't much to it. It might have been enough to start a campfire, and would surely not have felt good if it went off in your face, but it wasn't anything close to the beam of burning Janika or Justus could produce.

"He hasn't been through any typical Santa training, has he?" Bertram asked.

"We only found him a few days ago. Things have been busy since then," Randolph explained. "He's only technically my apprentice as of now."

"Wait," Daniel said. "I'm your apprentice?"

"Quiet," said Randolph. "Try again. This time, imagine a shape that you can focus the energy on. Something that will reach-"

Before Randolph could finish his thought, Daniel focused on a shape and tried again to produce fire. This time, it worked a lot better. A gout of flame that was razor thin, a few inches wide, and just over two feet long appeared, then flickered, and disappeared. Daniel whooped with delight.

Randolph and Bertram stared. Janika stared. Justus looked on without emotion.

"See what happens when you don't start these whelps off right?" Bertram asked.

Randolph gave him a sidelong look.

Daniel said, "Holy shit I can make a fire sword!"

Bertram nodded. "Yep, he's your apprentice all right,"

"It'll have to do for now," Randolph said. "We train to use beams because the distances they can cover are so important. We'll have to work on that training with you later."

Daniel tried again. This time, as he focused and used his magic word, (*shit!*) he swung his arm at a tree about three inches in diameter. The sword appeared, then flickered and went away again. The tree fell over, sliced neatly in half.

Daniel screamed and jumped up and down with delight. "Fire sword!" he yelled. "I can make a fucking fire sword!"

Randolph sighed.

"War is hell," Bertram observed.

"All right, let's try using some of Justus's defensive work now," Randolph said.

For the next few hours, they practiced. Daniel got better at keeping his fire sword alight for longer after a lot more tries, but he wasn't able to lengthen it or turn it into a beam like everyone else could. He wasn't too bad at making a shield with his other hand, and the beauty of the magical sword and shield approach is neither weighed anything.

Daniel tested the flame sword against the shimmering translucent area of his shield. The shield repelled the sword, but there was the sense of pain there when he tried it. What must it have been like for Justus when all those bullets were hitting the shield he created for Muromets back down by the river?

After some more practice with attack and defense spells, Bertram said, "Not too bad." Then, "So what's our plan? I assume these troops are part of a diversion?"

"Actually, I was rather thinking we would be the diversion," said Randolph. "The moment we start using magic, all of Krampus's forces should come boiling out of whatever crevices he's hiding them in. That should free up a few of the rest of us to get inside. Who better to do that than a fighter/healer, a teleporter, and a gun-toting redneck?"

"Hey," said Chris.

"Yes?" said Randolph.

Chris paused. "I guess I don't have a problem with that," he said.

Randolph raised his hand, palm up, for Bertram's benefit. You see?

"So it's just going to be you and me against the entire magical forces of Krampus?" Bertram asked.

"Well," said Randolph. "We are the highest ranking wizards in the world. I'm sure you feel like I do sometimes, which is that you've stored countless years of knowledge you'll never get to use because there simply aren't enough enemies at hand to warrant it. This time, you won't have that problem."

"Hmm," said Bertram. Then he raised his left hand like he was going to karate chop the air. He yelled "Motherfucker, shit!" On the "motherfucker," a thin purple beam of energy at least a meter wide appeared in the air, shooting directly out of Bertram's hand. Daniel couldn't see how far away the beam ended. For all he knew it went into space. It cut through the tops of probably two dozen trees. Each one jumped into the air a foot or so from the force of being cut. But when Bertram got to the "shit" part, he'd already changed his motion. The tree tops that had just been severed slammed back down into the trunks, appearing exactly as they had before.

Daniel gaped at this display, as did Chris and Janika. Even Justus appeared impressed.

Bertram straightened his suit jacket.

"Holy shit," said Chris, drawing his words out to multiple extra syllables for emphasis.

"I guess I wouldn't mind kicking a little ass," said Bertram.

Randolph raised an eyebrow. "Quite."

CHAPTER 39

Chris got dressed in a bunch of black clothing that made him look like he was straight off a movie shoot. None of it appeared to fit correctly.

"Man I wish I hadn't got all this stuff from a bunch of fat guys," he said. "Can't hardly keep these pants up at all."

He found a pair of bright yellow suspenders to keep his tactical pants up and had to settle for wearing them over the tactical vest he was also wearing, which was full of magazines for his rifles. He was wearing the smaller rifle slung to his chest. The bigger one had a two-piece strap that allowed it to be worn like a backpack, with the barrel pointing up into the air over his head.

"Nice suspenders," commented Janika, when Chris walked out of the house.

"I know they don't exactly fit but I can't have my pants around my ankles while I'm trying to kick Hitler in the dick," Chris said.

"You know Hitler is long dead? That's not who we are attacking."

Chris shrugged. "A major-league asshole is a major-league asshole," he said.

"Alright, people, it's afternoon here which means it's getting on for dark where we need to be. We will teleport in as a group, then Bertram, and myself will drop our rings so that the rest of you can teleport away. You'll will wait for the sound of the battle beginning, then let, say, five minutes pass, and begin making your way toward the entrance of the stronghold. With luck, the largest portion of Krampus's forces will be focused on us by that time."

"Can Muromets teleport?" Daniel asked.

"He should be able to, yes," said Randolph.

"What about me?" Chris asked.

"As long as someone holding a ring is touching you, you should teleport with the group," said Bertram.

Daniel looked up at the giant, standing over them. His face was, as usual, unreadable. He and Justus made quite a pair.

"Now, listen," said Randolph. "What you're looking for in the caves is a crystal. It should be about the size of a grape-fruit. If Chris shoots it with that giant gun of his, that should be enough to destroy it, which should seriously deplete Krampus's power."

"How do you know that's what we're looking for?" Daniel asked.

"Krampus's core magic is that he can crystallize belief. He spreads chaos, discontent, materialism. These things add to his power, then he uses magic to crystallize that energy to give him a greater store of power."

"So if we destroy the store of power, Krampus dies?" Daniel asked.

"It's not that easy," said Bertram. "He can't really die unless everyone in the world stops believing he exists, which, thanks to you damn kids and your dumbass Internet, ain't gonna happen."

"What if he's doing that storage magic when we get there?" Daniel asked.

"Then he'll stop and attack us instead," Randolph said.

Daniel nodded. "OK, good to know.

There was a moment of silence as everyone looked around at one another.

"Let's go," said Justus. He tugged on Muromet's flag kilt and the giant lifted him up onto his shoulders.

They went.

When they appeared, they were more or less where they'd popped into existence when they'd been looking for the entrance to the caves the first time. Randolph and Bertram each tucked their rings into their pocket. Justus tapped Muromets on the back and the giant put him down, but looked forlornly at him.

Justus patted the thor on the leg.

The giant made a moaning sound.

"Very well, Daniel, off you go," Randolph said.

Daniel concentrated on the whole group, then they were gone again, this time without Randolph and Bertram. They were a few hundred yards north. They began walking as a group, toward the wall of the valley which is where Randolph said the entrance to the cave system would be. Sure enough, in the distance, Daniel could see two large doors which were notched at the bottom so they could close over the train tracks that ran into the entrance. There was a lot of light there. He could see several mummies floating about.

"Geists," whispered Janika.

Daniel nodded.

"What?" Chris asked.

"Remember that mummy thing that was controlling your mind and got you hooked on meth?" Daniel asked.

"Yeah?"

"There are about a dozen of them down there."

"Bullshit," said Chris. He dropped the smaller rifle he'd been holding in his hands and it rode on the sling to which it was attached. Chris got the big rifle off his back and looked through the optics on the top. "Holy shit, you're right," he said. "Should I try to take a couple of them out?"

"No," said Janika. "We stick to the plan. Randolph and Bertram will be making a lot of noise shortly."

Justus nodded. "The plan," he said, simply.

They watched. A few moments later, there was a shout and a crackling sound. A bolt of lightning reached out to touch dark figures in the grass below, leaping from one to another as if they were each conductive. There were howls of pain, shrieks of anger. Bodies fell. The geists near the entrance headed toward the lightning.

A few seconds later, the two big doors opened. A giant stepped out. He looked similar to Muromets, but wasn't nearly as big. That was good news. But he was holding a chain that had to be as thick as a man, then end of which was attached to a cur the size of an elephant.

"Holy shit," said Chris. "That is one bigass motherfucking dog."

Around the giant's legs was a swarm of bodies. Geists and curs flooded out of the doors toward where Randolph and Bertram must be standing. The giant began walking forward; the enormous beast on the chain he held strained at it. Then he let go of the chain and the beast began to run, chain dragging behind. As the chain fell it slammed into several smaller curs, and there were yelps of pain.

The lightning flashed again. This time it arced between many more bodies, since they were so close together. It looked almost like a flashing electronic net with a geist or a cur at each node. Most of them went down immediately after the lightning flashed. Others staggered or howled, obviously very badly injured.

At the door, a large, red, horned figure appeared. Krampus himself. He roared, threw his head skyward, raised his hands. Magic swirled around his hands, then coalesced in front of him in a fiery blue column that grew. First it was the size of a fire hydrant, then a car stood on its end. It split at the bottom middle to form what looked like legs. It formed arms too, which ended in blue black fireballs, and a head with the suggestion of eye sockets and a gaping mouth. When Krampus was finished casting, he yelled to the fire monster and thrust his hands forward. The fire monster began to walk in the direction of the fire and light flashing up the valley.

"What the hell is that thing?" Daniel asked.

"I don't know, I've never seen one," said Janika.

"Can I shoot that red guy?" Chris asked.

"Plan," said Justus.

Krampus was following the giant flame monster, its enormous strides slow and face terrifying. The monster appeared to be screaming wordlessly.

"I think we go," said Justus. He stood.

Everyone else stood too. Chris slung his giant gun on his back again. "I wish now I hadn't brought this big-ass sniper rifle if I wasn't gonna be able to shoot anyone from our sniping position," he said.

"Leave it here, then," Daniel said.

"Hell no, this thing is worth a lotta money," Chris said. He shrugged into the straps and followed the rest of the group.

In the valley it looked like a combination fireworks display, laser show, and thunderstorm was taking place. The noise was terrific, with screams, thunderclaps, and bangs all occurring on top of one another. As attention-getting diversions went, it was top notch.

Daniel did not want to go through the doors in the rock

wall. He did not want to get close to them, in fact. Even though it seemed that every enemy who could possibly have boiled out of the caves had already done so, who knew what kind of horrors were within?

His fear grew as they got closer and closer, following Justus, who appeared to be untouched by concern. For all his talk about being an emotionless chasm, and as many problems as that must entail in everyday relationships, it must be awfully nice at a time like this.

They were at the door now. Inside, the rail tracks went around a bend. Nothing and no one greeted them. Daniel turned to look over his shoulder. The enormous flame monster was bringing a fist down to strike at something on the ground. There was a bright flash and a thunderclap, and the thing's arm was blown backward. It raised the arm to strike again.

He thought, silently, "Good luck, guys."

CHAPTER 40

The smell inside the cave was earthy, and there was a whiff of something that reminded Daniel of a dead animal beside a highway. The smell was faint. Perhaps he was imagining it.

Justus pressed a button on the wall and the large double doors began to close. They could still hear the clamor of battle outside through the doors as Justus hit a large metal release which caused a bolt to slam home, locking the doors from the inside. Daniel didn't know whether that would turn out to be a good idea or not, but it was part of the plan.

They hurried down the hallway. Chris pointed his rifle this way and that, presumably because he'd seen guys in movies do it that way. The smell was getting worse.

Ahead, the rock wall to the left side of the passage disappeared. The rail tracks continued, but it looked like there was an open space of some kind. As they drew closer, they could see there were what looked like white shapes. Justus motioned for quiet. They tiptoed as quietly as they could.

Just as they were about to reach the open area, a mummy stepped up onto the walkway and turned to shuffle down the tracks. Then it appeared to realize the group was behind it. It stopped, turned slowly.

It was wrapped in clean, white linen, like someone dressed as a mummy for a costume party.

It leaned forward toward the group and hissed with a rasping, bubbling noise, then began to shuffle toward them. Without thinking, Daniel rushed around from behind Justus, concentrated, then swung his hand and uttered a curt, "shit!" His fire sword appeared and sliced through the air. The mummy raised an arm, but the fire sword went through its arm without the slightest hitch. At the end of the arm and where the straps fell away, blue-black fire burned.

Daniel swung back the other way with the same spell, and this time the fire sword went through the mummy's middle section, cleaving it entirely in two. More black fire burned there, like the inside of a furnace. The mummy collapsed, was consumed by its own fire, leaving a pile of ashes behind.

Daniel gave a whoop, then turned back to look at the group.

They stared in horror over his shoulder. He turned to see what they were looking at.

To the left of the rail tracks was a large open area with a stone floor. Beds were lined in rows, far enough apart that someone could walk between them but also packed in closely enough to maximize the area. A few beds were empty. These had stained mattresses, as though someone who had just been wallowing in mud had lain down in the bed.

A small voice in Daniel's head warned that those stains might not be mud, which was supported by the fact that most of the beds had bodies lying in them. Some of the bodies were splotchy, black in places. Others were completely dark. One of these was being wrapped in white bandages by a white-bandaged mummy. He fought two competing urges: one to scream in horror and the other to retch.

"Geists," said Janika. Her voice trembled. "These are baby geists."

The mummies were looking up. One that was close by, wrapping bandages around a bloated black body, was staring at them. The body it was wrapping tried to move, shuddered, opened its mouth, flopped back to the bed.

"Fuck this," said Chris. He raised the rifle and fired. The closest mummy's head wobbled like a thrown water balloon and the thing crumpled.

The sound of the shot echoed aggressively off the walls of the chamber. Even though it was a huge space by cave standards, it was still enclosed rock wall.

Chris gave a little laugh, then began moving his barrel through the room from mummy to mummy. Some were shuffling in their direction, obviously intent on doing the group harm, but they were slow and easy to shoot. None made any effort to hide themselves or take cover. "Eat shit," Chris said, his cheek tight to the rifle as he fired. "And you too, pal," he said as he fired again. He began to walk sideways down the passage, firing into the shuffling forms of the mummies until there were none left standing.

The blacked body on the bed with wraps around one leg squirmed again, tried to rise once more. Chris shot it. It jerked and lay still.

"Yeah," said Chris. "Get some!"

"You have watched a lot of movies where people shoot one another, haven't you?" Janika asked.

"Sure as hell have," Chris said.

There was a terrific smash behind them that echoed up the tunnel and into the cavern.

"We gotta go find that crystal," said Janika.

There was another smash. This time the sounds of fighting outside got a little louder. Someone or something was smashing the door down. They turned and ran down the rail tracks, deeper into the caves. Ahead the passage opened again, this time into a cavern on both sides of the tracks. There were bowls scattered around the floor on the right, and a huge double door. The door on the right had a smaller door set into it with a window. Janika ran to it, looked through.

"Not this one!" she yelled.

There was also a double door in the far wall, straight ahead. Chris pulled on the massive iron ring in it. Nothing.

Daniel walked toward the doors Chris was trying to open. There was a crack between them. He could see beyond it, and was able to make out something of what the room looked like by moving his head side to side. It looked round, with a round raised area in the center. Everything looked pinkish inside, as if it were being lit by a child's night light. "I think I can handle this," he said. He closed his eyes, concentrated, reached a hand out to grab Chris by the shoulder.

Janika yelled "No!" but was cut off.

They teleported. Daniel ended up facing the stone pillar in the middle of the room. He expected to see a crystal in it. Indeed, the plinth had an angled hole in it as though it were meant to support something like a big crystal, but there was nothing in it. He reached a hand into it and felt around. Stone. Nothing else. He looked up. The room's ceiling was high overhead, hundreds of feet. At its apex was a tiny twinkle of light.

There was a shout from behind him. He turned.

Randolph and Bertram were there. They both whipped their heads around. Randolph was sweaty and holding one of his arms like his shoulder wasn't working properly. Bertram had a cut on his cheek from which a trickle of blood was leaking. Both had tears in their clothes in various places. Randolph's white shirt showed grass stains. His jacket was gone.

"You fool!" Randolph yelled. "You teleported us all. Back to the cave entrance, immediately!"

"I'm sorry," Daniel yelled, fear rising in his belly. "I forgot it would take us all!"

"Move us back, boy" yelled Bertram. "Now! Now!"

Daniel closed his eyes again and the group disappeared and reappeared in the mouth of the cave. The doors were smashed apart at the bottom and at the top corners but weren't totally open. A geist was floating through the gap at the bottom with a handful of curs right behind it. The geist directed a flaming ball at Bertram, but Justus threw up a protective shield that deflected the ball upward. It scorched the roof of the tunnel and dust filtered down.

Bertram cast a chain of lightning from his hands that searched the air, found the leading geist, then arced to the curs behind. The power of the spell rocked the air with a pressure wave that caused Daniel to stagger backwards.

Randolph too was casting again. He was aiming his fire at the top hole in the doors, where two big, black flaming balls kept trying to snake into them. Daniel realized these were the "hands" of the flaming monster that Krampus had conjured. When Randolph's beam of flame touched the hands they recoiled, but they were still burning away at the wood of the doors little by little.

Finally, the monster reached into the top of the doors from either side and gave them a mighty yank. There was a shriek of metal and the cracking of great timbers. The top of the door pulled down. Randolph hit the monster with a full beam of fire and it was obviously hurt, but not enough to break off the attack. It would only be a matter of seconds before the flame monster had the door completely torn away, and then it would come in and, eventually, kill them all.

"Take us back to the crystal room!" Randolph yelled. "We can destroy it!"

"It's no use," Daniel said. "There was nothing in there!"

"What?" Bertram yelled.

Daniel shook his head violently. "Nothing! There was a plinth but no crystal."

Through the flame monster's legs, Daniel could see the red figure of Krampus, watching the battle and laughing. He walked forward at a measured pace, his fists on his red furred hips.

CHAPTER 41

The flame monster had the doors torn completely open, now. Krampus twiddled fingers at the thing and it was still. He strolled toward the mouth of the cave, triumphant smile on his face. "Can I assume," he said. "That you idiots have been to my crystal room and found nothing?"

No one replied. Randolph did his best to straighten his torn clothes.

Krampus laughed again. "Oh, this is too rich," he said. He walked closer, just a few feet away. "Just entirely too rich for my poor black heart to bear. If only you knew how close you were, hmm? And yet, here you are. Ah well. I suppose I'll have my friend destroy you now-"

He was cut off by Janika, who cast a beam of flame at him. He flicked the tree branch he held in his hand and the beam disappeared. He laughed.

"Yes, please do try your magic against mine, little Santa," Krampus said. "You will find, as your masters did, that it might work against older versions of my magic, but not against me, or against my latest creations."

"If you mean the geists in the chamber down the hall, we killed them," Daniel said.

Krampus waved this away. "A trivial matter when compared with my latest work." He indicated the flame monster standing in the mouth of the cave with a wave of a hand. "Do you like him?"

"No," said Janika.

Krampus laughed again. He put a hand on his belly as he laughed. "Fair enough. I suppose you wouldn't."

Bertram dusted himself off. "Don't listen to this asshole, team," he said. "We did good work here today."

"Indeed," Randolph agreed.

"Not quite good enough, though, was it?" Krampus asked in a mocking tone. He pointed a finger. A bolt of energy shot out of it toward Janika, but Justus cast a shield quickly that deflected the bolt.

Krampus slapped one of this thighs with a hand and made a frustrated grunting sound. "Let's see you divert this next one. What do you say to that, eh?" He twiddled his fingers at the flame monster again.

It ducked its head and stepped inside the cave, its empty flaming eye sockets and mouth agape. It raised an arm as though it would bring a fist down on the group and destroy them all in a single blow.

There was an ear-splitting crack, and the earth shook. Everyone put their arms out to help maintain their balance, including Krampus who stumbled backward. His eyes were wide. He clutched at his chest.

The flame monster overhead flamed out with a bang, and there was a rush of hot, stinking wind.

"No!" yelled Krampus. He gritted his teeth with rage, then threw his head back and howled, still clutching at his chest. "Nooo!" He charged at the group, which was terrifying. Even if his flame monster had dissipated somehow, which it seemed to have done, Krampus was still an enormous beast who could do serious physical damage, especially with those horns.

Bertram cast his lightning spell again as Krampus charged. Krampus deflected it easily. Other spells bounced off him as if they'd never been cast.

Justus stepped forward and threw a punch that started at his feet, traveled smoothly up his legs to his hips, then through his powerful body and to the balled hammer of his fist. It hit Krampus in the middle of his face and the beast stumbled, dazed, eyes apparently trying to look at one another.

"So you've lost your magic," said Justus. He whirled, then kicked his foot out and connected with Krampus's gut.

"Huggh," Krampus grunted as the air left his lungs.

"You don't need magic to fight, red man," said Justus. He threw a jab to distance the monster, then followed it up with an uppercut that again relied on his legs and hips for strength.

Krampus's great horned head jerked backwards so he was looking upward. He staggered backward yet again, went down on one knee.

"Get up, red man. We are fighting now, not resting," said Justus. "Maybe put your sticks down and throw your hands."

Krampus's huge face was bleeding. He looked like he'd never been more surprised in his life. He looked at the bough he kept in his hands as if he'd never seen it before. Then his face darkened. He twiddled his fingers at Justus, and Justus staggered, fell backwards.

"I haven't lost all my magic," said Krampus, rising. He moved his arms so that the thick chain that normally rested over his neck hung loose. "But if you're determined to find out what kind of damage I can do without magic..." He began swinging the chain around now. It was so heavy that it caused him to have to brace his body against the swinging momentum. He was looming over Justus now. "...then I am happy," he said, grunting with the effort of spinning the chain, "to oblige!"

Krampus brought his arms up over his head, spinning the chain high into the air. He was going to bring it down on Justus and the result would be utterly terrifying. One of those chain links moving at that speed could smash through flesh and body — even someone Justus's size — with no problem at all. The whole chain would be utter destruction.

As the chain reached the highest point of its arc, Janika screamed, "Justus!"

Daniel screamed, "No!"

An enormous hand caught the chain at its apex and used it to lift Krampus off the ground. Muromets, bleeding from a hundred wounds and smeared with dirt, spun his enormous body around holding Krampus on the end of his chain, then, after a few spins to gain speed, let go of the chain, sending the monster high into the night air. Krampus tumbled into the blackness and was swallowed by it. His screams disappeared into the air, too.

Muromets made a cooing sound in his throat, bent down, picked Justus up off his back, and set the man on his feet. Then the giant sat down, hard. The ground shook with the impact.

CHAPTER 42

"E veryone ok?" Bertram asked. Everyone looked around.

"You both look terrible," said Janika. "We should be asking you if you're OK."

"I might be," said Randolph. "But this suit is ruined."

"Hey," said Daniel, looking around. "Where's Chris?"

RATHER THAN TRYING TO TELEPORT AGAIN, DANIEL AND Janika walked back down the hall, past the mummy growing area to the large chamber with the closed door at the end of the hall. Only now, the doors were riddled with bullet holes. They were rattling as though someone from the other side were slamming into them, trying to get them to open.

Daniel yelled, "Chris, you in there?"

The rattling stopped.

"Yeah, maybe. Who's asking?"

"It's me, Daniel,"

Daniel put his face up to the crack between doors and was met with a view of one of Chris's eyes.

"Ya left me in here, you dumb shit," Chris said.

"Stand to the side, Chris," said Janika.

When he'd said he was out of the way, Janika cast a beam of fire that blazed through the wood of the door, making a neat round hole with blackened edges. Whatever magic had protected them had apparently dissipated.

Inside, the room where Chris had been trapped was dark.

"Hey," said Daniel, "Wasn't there light in here before?"

"Yeah," said Chris. "Ugly pink light overhead. I shot just before that earthquake. Everyone else OK? Are we still doin' war?"

⚜

"So you mean to tell me," said Randolph. He paused. Blinked.

They were back at the cave mouth, now. Justus had finished seeing to Muromets and was healing Randolph and Bertrand.

Randolph started again. "You mean to tell me that you shot what you thought was the overhead lighting fixture with that enormous rifle?"

Chris shrugged. "Well, hell. I didn't get to fire the 50 at all and it's cool as fuck. So I'm stuck in this dumbass room with this pink light all around. I look up and it's coming from some kinda tiny light fixture thing pretty far away and I think well, hell, I can hit that with this rifle for sure. So. Yeah. I shot it."

Randolph stared in wonderment.

"So that was the crystal?" Janika asked.

"Apparently so," said Randolph. "Chris you saved all of us, including yourself."

Chris shrugged again. "I just wanted to shoot this rifle one time."

Bertram said, "I guess Krampus must have thought his best bet was to hide the crystal in plain sight. Who knows what kind of magical protection it had, if we'd tried to ascend that shaft to get to it?"

"Who indeed," agreed Randolph.

"Where's Krampus now?" Daniel asked.

"He'll be back," said Bertram. "He'll recover, regroup, find some other way to come at us."

"What are we going to do?" Daniel asked.

Bertram shrugged. "Same thing," he said. "To start with we need to get us a new HQ."

"Yes," Randolph agreed. "And you, Daniel, need some training."

"Hey, I want some training," said Chris. "Can I help fight these assholes?"

Randolph looked at Bertram.

"We'll consider it," Bertram said. "We don't really do guns, but you've certainly proven yourself useful today."

"I think we talk some other time," said Justus. "Everyone needs rest."

"Where should we go to rest?" Daniel asked.

"I'm thinking a beach," said Randolph. "Preferably one that has some delicious cocktails and women my own age."

"Sounds like Florida to me," said Chris.

"No Florida," said Randolph.

RANDOLPH ELECTED TO BE DROPPED OFF IN SAN DIEGO. HE sent Daniel a photo via text a few days later of himself in a men's bikini style swimsuit holding a very tall colorful cocktail in one hand and a smiling older woman under the other arm.

Janika texted often to ask how he was doing settling back into school. She communicated that Justus said hello, but Daniel doubted if the big man really said anything.

Chris also was dropped off back at his house with Muromets, who crawled into the barn again and was snoring in minutes. Chris would go on to report that the giant moped for days. Chris thought this was due to missing Justus.

His dorm room and school life seemed like the most boring things in the world to Daniel now. He kept his gold ring on his body at all times, and would reach his hand into his pocket to feel it occasionally.

It was decided that the order needed a few months to recover and recuperate and there was no good reason for Daniel not to be at school during that time, especially given that that was where he was supposed to be.

But after school and on weekends, he would teleport himself with Janika and Justus to various spots for fun.

"It's kind of sad, what happened to the Santas," said Daniel, sitting on a bench overlooking Notre Dame in Paris, watching tourists take photos. "All those years of building themselves up and then this."

Janika shrugged. "We'll be back." She gave Daniel a warm smile.

Though he had never considered himself much of a smooth operator, something about the moment, about the smile she gave him, gave Daniel the confidence to reach his arm up over Janika and place it on the back of the bench. He wasn't hugging her, exactly, but she was technically within the sphere of his personal space. She smiled at him again, then sat back so that she was resting against his arm.

"What do you think, Justus?" Daniel asked. "Can we rebuild?"

"I think," said the big man, looking away. "You are moving that arm or I am tearing it off and throwing it into the river."

Daniel laughed. Janika laughed. Justus turned and showed Daniel his face, stern as ever, without a trace of humor on it. Daniel moved his arm.

Then Justus rumbled a laugh, lightly swatted at Daniel's leg. "Don't worry," he said. "I like you."

Daniel summoned every ounce of his courage, lifted his arm again, an arm he might shortly be watching splash into the Seine, and placed it behind Janika. She leaned into him.

Yes. Krampus would rebuild.

But so would the Santas.

THE END

Hi there. Your author Jim Hodgson here. Thanks for reading Santa vs. Krampus. This book combines a couple of ideas I have been interested in exploring for a few years now. I hope you liked it. If you did, tell a friend!

I loved writing in this world so we'll be seeing more of these characters.

It means a lot to independent authors like myself to have your support. Check out my web site at http://jimhodgson.com and maybe join my excellent mailing list. If you have a moment, leave an honest review on what you just read. It all helps.

I thank you, my wife thanks you, the universe at large thanks you. Trust me about the universe. I asked it, which was pretty complicated I can tell you.

Drop me a line any time at jim@jimhodgson.com.

Made in the USA
Lexington, KY
18 December 2017